BY THE SEA

BY PETER LEVINE

ISBN: 978-1-969021-45-9 (ebook)
ISBN: 978-1-969021-46-6 (Paperback)
ISBN: 978-1-969021-47-3 (Hardcover)
Library of Congress Control Number: 2026932356

IN LOVING MEMORY OF
MY MOTHER PEARL
AND
FOR MY GRANDCHLDREN
BEN AND LILY

Author's Note

If my mother were alive today, here in New York, she would be 110 years old. An urban warrior. Like the bent and crippled old women, walkers or canes their companions, who brave the streets and the traffic and the noise and the dirt on their daily outings for a quart of milk, a banana, maybe even a pack of cigarettes, the feeble, at times leading each other, stopping the hullabaloo around them dead in its tracks. Undaunted and oblivious to danger, they stay the course until they reach the curb on the other side, linked together by flesh, metal, and wood, safety in numbers even as their numbers steadily dwindle.

My mother never got the chance. She died in 1973 at the age of 63. Cancer claimed her, only a few hours after she had learned of the death of her first son and only months after her husband of almost forty years predeceased her from another version of the same disease.

I told her that her son, my brother, had died. I held her hand as she heaved her last breath, carefully taking off her wedding band lest it be stolen by a nurse or by the mortuary - her sister's advice - a ring now proudly worn by my daughter. And here I am, back in Brooklyn, now almost twenty years older than my mother when she died, married sixty years, enjoying a retirement my parents longed for but never quite managed. Not in the Florida of their dreams but on the very urban turf they hoped to flee.

In different ways over the years, I have written about my family, with the emphasis on my father. Works of history, fiction, the very rare poem, and now plays, that trace our past and my constant effort to make peace and sense of our world, achieving it more frequently now, even if at times, I still struggle with its neurotic remnants.

But my mother never got her due. Not just her, but the generation of women she represented strong, bright, energetic people who worked, took care of a home, cooked, cleaned, shopped, laundered, and raised children.

How to capture that woman her dreams, desires, fantasies, disappointments, the what ifs of her life, her heroes, heroines, how she felt about the burdens of family, what her joys and regrets might have been, has inspired me to create this story. I hope she would approve.

P.L.

Chapter One

H e did not mean to stalk her. It wasn't in his nature. That's not how he had been brought up. Not this Brooklyn boychik, straight out of Flatbush, a Momma's boy who considered everything west of the Hudson River, the South. He of limited horizons and little interest in anything that could not be found within the confines of the five boroughs, even including Staten Island, which normally, he did not.

It began quite innocently. Five-thirty on a late Thursday afternoon. The usual rush of people exiting the office building where he worked at pell-mell, helter-skelter, all heading through the revolving doors that emptied onto Eighth Avenue - off to home, to dinner with friends, crowded subways and buses - the countless options the city offered accustomed to the pulsing urban rhythms that defined their daily lives. Barely missing a beat, they surged through the doors, alternate merging as if cars on a highway, one person to each compartment, keeping a constant pace to avoid unfortunate collisions. That is where he first encountered her, several steps behind, as she waited for her moment to wade into the circular sweep.

Actually, encounter is too active a word to describe it. It was the simple sight of her, his close proximity to her presence even as she pushed through the doors and headed uptown, that so attracted him. Caught up in the moment, he decided to follow her as she walked headlong into the throngs of people headed downtown towards Penn Station on their journeys home.

He kept his distance, always a good ten steps behind, not that she was likely to notice anything out of the ordinary in the usual crush of people out and about in the city during rush hour.

The air was crisp, good weather for walking, which turned out to be fortuitous as the woman continued uptown through Hell's Kitchen, heading towards Columbus Circle. At West 54th Street she turned east towards Broadway, and then, without warning (not that he should have expected one), she turned into #554, an office building on the south side of the street, two doors down from Studio 54.

He watched her enter, not sure how to proceed. Should he follow her? After all, she had no idea who he was, or that he had been stalking her for the last twenty minutes. Or would his own nervous excitement somehow give him away? What was the point of it all? Was it purely sexual, even though he had yet to see her face? Why had he pursued her in the first place? Would he blurt something out that he would live to regret?

All this doubt, hesitation, and confusion occupied him no more than a few seconds. But by the time he decided to push through the lobby door and head towards the elevator, she had disappeared, along with whomever else might have been waiting to go up.

He watched the numbers at the top of the lintel as the elevator ascended on the odd chance that they might at least tell him what floor she got off on. As luck would have it, the elevator stopped on three different floors: the third, fifth, and seventh - before beginning its descent.

Disappointed but undeterred, he considered his options. He could wait in the lobby until she reappeared from wherever she had gone. He could give up the chase and go home, at least for this day. There might even be time for him to get in his daily run around Prospect Park before it got dark. The Q train was only a few blocks away. Or, he thought, he could begin to consider where she might have gone by examining the building directory which unfortunately listed occupants alphabetically rather than by floor.

It took him a few minutes to compile a dossier of the businesses located on each of the three floors at which the elevator had stopped. Interspersed among the ten different doctors' offices covering the spectrum from podiatry to proctology, they included a printing company, three accounting firms, two lawyers' offices, and one acting studio, The Actors' Friend, that shared the seventh floor with a gynecologist and a company mysteriously listed as Imported Delights.

Eliminating the proctologist was a no brainer. The printing company seemed unlikely. Given the quick pace and easy style with which she walked, so too the podiatrist. Everyone else was still in the game. He looked at his watch. If he hurried, he still had time to squeeze in his run. Who knew how long she would be? He headed towards the subway. Surely, there would be another day to continue the hunt.

So immersed had he been in his work, that he had neglected to notice a steady stream of a dozen or so men and women, mostly in their late twenties and early thirties, who entered the building and headed up to the seventh floor, a missed opportunity that might have helped him narrow his search.

Chapter Two

By the time Paul Goodwin headed home to Brooklyn, Sally Martinelli had hung up her coat, changed her shoes, and sat ready in Studio B of The Actors' Friend, waiting for her class to begin. "An Introduction to Improv," the come-on had announced, once a week for ten weeks on a pay as you go basis, thirty dollars for a two-hour class, a New York bargain no matter how you sliced it.

This was her second time in attendance. She had no interest in becoming an actor, a comedian, or a public speaker. Simple, human contact was all she sought. She knew no one in the class and had yet to volunteer, too self-conscious to participate beyond the simplest repetition drills that required only minimal speech.

She had made it through the mirroring exercises - no need for verbal communication here, just ape whatever your partner offered with his or her body parts, but tonight, she knew, would be different. She needed to overcome her hesitancy here, in this unfamiliar place, so far removed from the tragedy that had shaped her recent past even as it provided the financial wherewithal to begin again.

To begin again. That's what Noah would have wanted. That was her mantra, what she continually told herself, as she systematically disengaged from the life she shared with him in East Lansing, Michigan after his unexpected death from a cycling accident six months earlier, no more than a mile from the home that they had lived in for close to twenty years.

A skilled, experienced rider, as always, Noah was wearing his helmet when the accident occurred. But his Masi Gran Criterium was no match for the pick-up truck that side-swiped him on Marsh Road in the early morning hours of a sweltering, sunny, summer day. He flipped over the front of his bike, went air-borne, and landed on his head and left shoulder only a few feet from where his bike lay in tangled ruins. The driver of the truck, who remained on the scene, called 911 and went to Noah's aid. He told the police that he never saw him. Dazed and bruised but fully conscious, Noah sat up on the ground and was able, with some assistance, to walk to the EMT truck, which arrived within ten minutes after the collision.

The EMTs took his vital signs, placed his left arm in an air cast and headed towards Sparrow Hospital in Lansing.

"Looks like a broken collar bone, Doc, we're taking you in," one of them said, having recognized him as Dr. Noah Lipson, a neurologist affiliated with Lansing Neurology, the preeminent local neurology group whose doctors were frequent visitors to Sparrow.

"No hurry," Noah replied. "I'm doing fine."

Those were the last words he ever spoke. By the time the ambulance turned onto Grand River Avenue and headed downtown, blood began pouring out of his ears. His breathing became labored, and he collapsed into a coma from which he never awoke.

The official autopsy report indicated that the meninges, the membranes surrounding his brain, had burst, resulting in catastrophic damage that left him instantly brain dead. He lingered in this vegetative state for a week, kept alive by every medical device imaginable, while his partners refused to accept the inevitable. Sally knew from her many conversations with Noah that he would have had no desire to live this way, even for a moment. It was only when she demanded that his colleagues take him off all life support, that they finally acceded.

Now here she was. Back in the city of her birth, one she had abandoned years ago. One she no longer knew. No old friends to connect with, her parents long gone, an only child who fell in love during her sophomore year at Barnard with a medical student at Physicians and Surgeons and never looked back. She spent the next thirty years of her life with Noah, as his career took them first to Baltimore, then St. Louis, and finally to his East Lansing practice, where they lived happily before his unexpected death. Noah pursued the work he loved while she worked on her poetry, taught an occasional course at the local community college, and enjoyed the benefits of living in a Big Ten college town with reasonable access to the arts, and of course, more big-time college sports than she could stomach.

But place mattered little to her. It was her daily life with Noah that was at the heart of her existence and well-being. Once that abruptly ended, the decision to move was less momentous than it might have seen.

Money was no issue. A double-indemnity accident life insurance policy that Noah had taken out when he began working in Michigan and his share of the practice secured her financial future. She had no close friends, just some casual acquaintances easily acquired in a mid-western landscape and just as easily left behind.

Left behind as well would be the constant reminders of her life with Noah and of its tragic end, reason enough in her mind, to move on. More than once, as she grappled with her decision, she was reminded of the passage in Gabriel Garcia Marquez's *Love in the Time of Cholera*, when Fermina Daza, one of the novel's chief protagonists, ponders the death of her husband of many years: "Everything that belonged to her husband made her weep again: his tasseled slippers, his pajamas under the pillow, the space of his absence on the dressing table mirror, his own odor on her skin. A vague thought made her shudder. 'The people one loves should take all their things with them when they die.'" Noah had not been that considerate, so Sally acted on her own.

New York was a logical choice. Aside from East Lansing, it was the only place she had lived in for more than a few years. It was where she grew up and went to public school and college. Now, almost fifty, she returned to a city far different from the one she had known, hoping to begin again. That's why she had signed up for the class. Now it was time to practice what she preached.

Jim Horton, the class's bespectacled, rotund, fifty-something, curly- haired instructor, called the class to order by reminding his students of the basic rules of short form improv that they were about to explore:

"Even though these games are meant to be short and quick, don't forget to create an actual scene. Make sure it has a beginning and an end. Above all, listen and respond. Be bold, be yourself and play with confidence. Alright, any questions?"

"Be yourself?" Sally thought. "If only I knew what that meant!"

"Alright then. Let's get going," Horton continued. "No need to volunteer, everyone gets their turn, like it or not." A few students giggled nervously as Horton proceeded.

"First up for a game of 'He Said, She Said.' Let's see…" He looked over his class list and called out: "Sally Martinelli and Jose Santiago. Come on down!"

Jose, a young Puerto Rican man in his early twenties, bounded to his feet and took center stage, eagerly facing his classmates. With far less enthusiasm, Sally joined him. Neither had a clue of what was to follow.

"It's a simple game," Horton explained. "Each player describes an action they want from their partner. For example, Sally might say to Jose, 'I'd like to talk to you, Jose.' Referring to Sally, Jose might continue the thought by adding, referring to Sally, 'she said, putting her hand on her hips.' Sally then has to carry out that physical action. Then it's Sally's turn to tell Jose what physical action should accompany his response. And so it continues. Got it?"

Jose laughed and practiced snapping an imaginary bull whip while Sally stood quietly, a bit dumbfounded. Nor, she noticed, by the looks of some of her classmates' faces, was she alone.

"I'm not sure," she muttered.

"No problem," Horton responded. "Let's just give it a go. Jose, why don't you begin? Face each other and pay attention. Just let yourselves go!"

"I'd like to talk to you, Sally," Jose began, choosing the path of least resistance.

Sally responded in kind: "He said, putting her hands on his hips."

Jose looked perplexed, and Horton intervened. "Are you sure that's what you want, Sally?"

Sally thought for a moment, saw the problem, and corrected herself. "No, I meant his hands on his hips."

Jose smiled and did as instructed. So far, so good, she thought. But then her partner countered: "'All right,' she said, while sticking her index fingers in her ears, rolling them around, and then smelling them."

Sally looked at Jose in disbelief. Not that she hadn't, at one time or another, done the very action he demanded. But never in front of other people! People she barely knew!

"Come on, Sally," Horton urged. "Remember to be bold and confident!"

"Fuck you," Sally thought, as she felt her face redden. "You want bold, I'll give you bold!"

"Fine!" Sally said, suddenly, without thinking, transforming herself into Sister Mary Katherine Gallagher, Molly Shannon's beloved nun from *Saturday Night Live*. As her classmates cheered her on, she emphatically and dramatically smelled her fingertips, then, overwhelmed by the odor, crashed in a heap onto the floor. From her prone position, she blurted out: "And he made the suggestion, while dropping his pants, and mooning Mr. Horton!"

"Mooning?" Que pasa? I'm not sure what that is," Jose exclaimed.

"Game over, I win!" Sally declared and returned to her seat, acknowledging the applause offered by several classmates.

"Sally," Horton interrupted. "Don't you think that was…"

"You asked for Bold."

"Yes, but…"

"No buts about it," Sally countered.

"And no pun intended! You go, girl!" a Black woman named Gloria chimed in.

Sally smiled and sat back in her chair.

"Alright, let's move on. Who's next?" Horton resumed. And so, it went for the next forty minutes as the other students paired up and went through the same drill. Then, after a ten-minute break, the class picked up again, with a new exercise.

"This is one of my favorite games," Horton announced. "It's a chance to do a short scene involving three players. It's called 'The Funeral Service.' Player One, at the suggestion from the audience, acts out getting killed. It could be anything. Cancer, suicide, a bike accident, whatever. Then the other two players mourn their friend by talking about his life. At any point, the dead person can jump up and act out whatever moment his friends are describing. Then, at the end of the scene, the dead person gets back in his coffin."

"Death should only be that simple," Gloria snorted.

"Alright, let's see who goes first." Horton looked down at his list and called out: "Gloria, Bill and..."

Even as her name began to form on Horton's lips, Sally grabbed her coat and shoes and was out the door.

Chapter Three

Paul toweled off quickly, ran a brush through his thick, black hair, slipped on a fresh pair of dungarees, a polo shirt, and his Asics Gel Nimbus running shoes. He had two pairs, one for putting in his miles in the park, the other, just for everyday use, both replaced every six months like clockwork, the date of purchase, the mileage, and the times of his daily runs all recorded in his daily calendar that he picked up each year for free at Thanksgiving at Sahadi's on Atlantic Avenue his favorite place to shop for bulk food, chocolate and Middle Eastern delights. He checked his watch, grabbed his fleece and headed out the door and down the stoop of his parlor floor brownstone apartment on Ninth Street, right off of Prospect Park West.

It was just past 7 P.M. He had called Louise to tell her that he would be late and not to hold dinner up on his account.

"No problem, honey. Pearl's still napping. Take your time. You'll get here when you get here."

Louise. When had she not been a part of his life? From as far back as he could recall, every Tuesday this large, warm, boisterous, Black woman would come all the way from Bed-Stuy by bus and arrive at his mother's home promptly at 8 A.M. to clean their Junior Four apartment. Mostly, she aired out the pillows and changed the bed sheets. She also dusted what had already been dusted and washed the linoleum floors that already sparkled, all of which his mother had done the night before. She also made him lunch when he came home from P.S. 255, his elementary school, only a few short blocks away down Avenue S.

"What you want for lunch today?" She would ask, rattling off the list of options his mother had left in the refrigerator to choose from. In the end, it was always the same: a BLT on white toast with plenty of mayonnaise, two Mallomars and a glass of milk.

Even after he had moved out on his own, they stayed in touch. She carried his high school graduation picture in his wallet. When he was in college, she had a heart attack. He visited her at Kings County Hospital. She cried when she saw him.

"What you want for lunch today?" she laughed weakly. Her mouth was parched and dry. He held a cup of water to her lips while she sipped through a straw.

Louise recovered, continued her daily grind as a "cleaning girl," but as soon as her Social Security kicked in, she retired. And when Pearl, Paul's mother, had a stroke that left her physically unable to fend for herself, he asked Louise if she would move into her apartment, the same one that he had grown up in, to become her caretaker. That had been ten years ago. They had been together ever since.

Louise Barnett and Pearl Goodwin were not exactly "two peas in a pod." Louise was a proud, tough, Black woman who migrated North from her Alabama roots. Never married, she had been on her own ever since. Pearl, almost a decade older, was pushing eighty, a short, white, Jewish woman, the daughter of Russian immigrants, once a schoolteacher, long widowed, and always the loving mother of her only son. But somehow, they managed together, forming a friendship and a reliance on each other, despite the occasional disagreements that were a part of their bond.

Such was the state of affairs when Paul arrived. After hugging and kissing both women, the three sat down at the kitchen table to share a roast chicken dinner that Pearl had proudly prepared from the groceries that Louise had shopped for on Avenue U that afternoon.

"So, did you see who died yesterday?" Pearl asked her son, as she passed him the bowl of overcooked canned green beans.

"No, Mom, I didn't."

"What you read those damn obituaries for. They always upset you. And a woman your age should not be getting upset."

Pearl gave Louise a look at the reference to her age and continued: "If I don't see my name, I know I'm still alive."

"Least not dead," Louise replied.

"There's a difference?"

"Depends on the day," Louise chuckled.

"Anyway," Pearl continued, "did you see who died?"

"Who died, Mom?" Paul asked.

"Consuelo Velazquez."

"Who's that?" Louise asked.

"You don't know? Consuelo Velazquez, the songwriter?"

Paul and Louise both shook their heads.

"I don't believe it! She was 88 years old. And in 1941 she wrote *Besame Mucho*, one of the greatest hits of all time."

"Never heard of it." Louise said.

Besame Mucho? You don't remember?"

"Remembering ain't one of my strong suits."

Before Paul could respond, Pearl broke into melodic song: "Besame, Besame mucho. Each time I bring you a kiss I hear music divine/Besame, Besame mucho...DaDaDa, DaDaDa, DaDaDa, DadaDa, Da. You don't remember it?"

"Sounds like you don't either."

"The last line always gave me trouble. Paulie, you remember it now?"

"Yes, Ma, "Paul laughed. "You sometimes sang it to me when I was a little kid."

"Everybody and his uncle recorded it. Dave Brubeck (Louise whistled the first few bars of *Take Five*, Nat King Cole (she crooned in with *Unforgettable*), The Platters (in full voice now, belting out "Oh yes. I'm the Great Pretender.)"

Pearl gave Louise a nasty look and played her ace card: "Even Steve Lawrence and Edie Gormé!"

"Who?" Louise asked.

Pearl looked at her in disbelief. "Steve and Edie! Big stars. They were always on TV. Ed Sullivan, The Carol Burnett Show, Gary Moore...."

"White?" Louise queried.

"Yes."

"Never heard of them."

"What about Dave Brubeck? He's white!" Pearl shot back.

"Jazz is jazz. That boy still alive?"

"Mom, Louise, please stop, you're killing me," Paul implored jokingly.

Louise laughed. "OK, you win. You take your *Besame Mucho*. I'll stick with Billy Holiday and *Strange Fruit*."

"Who's that?" Pearl innocently asked.

"She knows who she is," Louise retorted. "We're just playing with each other. That's what we do. But enough of us. How you're doing, honey?"

"I'm doing," Paul responded.

"Anything romantic to report?" Pearl inquired.

"You'll be the first to know," Paul answered, even though he knew that at this point in his life, his mother's probe was merely perfunctory. Long ago she had resigned herself that her son would remain single, if not celibate, despite all the goodness and wonder she saw in him. If only she knew that he had spent the late afternoon stalking a woman, he did not know but whom he remained determine to pursue.

Chapter Four

S o much for The Actors' Friend. A whim at best, Sally mused, as she walked uptown the next day from her apartment in the John Adams, a white brick, post -World War Two building located on Sixth Avenue between 12th and 13th Streets.

Not so The Writer's Place, the serious business that defined her daily existence. Four afternoons a week, Monday through Thursday, from 1 to 5, she rented a cubicle there on the 8th floor of 520 Eighth Avenue, the very building where Paul Goodwin first saw her, to practice her craft.

Sally had been writing poetry since she was a little girl. On her own, with no help or guidance from teachers or parents. She took pleasure in the way words sounded, the music they created, the rhythms they produced, and the meaning they conveyed. Not that she could have articulated such insights as a child. It was just something that she enjoyed.

Puberty intervened, and her interest waned. There were boys, parties, a brief flirtation with running track in high school, and then on to college, followed by her life with Noah. It was not until she returned to Brooklyn when she was twenty-eight, to clean out her mother's apartment after her death, that her interest was rekindled.

Going through her mother's roll-top desk, drawer by drawer, discarding old bills, restaurant menus and the like, she discovered a trove of her poems that her mother had diligently saved. Scattered among the scraps of paper that contained her hand-written verse were her only two published efforts one written for a fourth-grade elementary school collection and the other penned when she was fourteen that had appeared in a collection of adolescent poems about the environment.

Sitting on her mother's bed, she read them out loud, just as she used to do when she first wrote them:

"The Arglefarg"

The Arglefarg is a mile tall,

So, he has to make sure he doesn't fall.

The Arglefarg has a huge tail,

So big it's the size of a whale.

The Arglefarg has a giant head of hair, So many planes and helicopters get stuck in there.

But the Arglefarg gets very lonely with his head in the sky,

For no one is with him when he eats his pie.

"Well, at least it rhymes!" she smiled.

Not so "So This Is Freedom," that appeared in *the Anthology of New York High School Poetry a few years later:*

7 years old, I belonged to two families.

My family at home and my Tree family.

My tree family, inside my favorite birch, small, but never overlooked.

The walls, a faint misty lilac, the carpet shaggy and white, grayed with age and the mess of my being there.

14 years old, double a lifetime, of knowledge, of wisdom, of suffering.

Every footstep, a mountain climbed.

Every heartbeat, a race run.

Every conversation, a weekend of obnoxious partying.

All purpose, lost.

My shadow stalking me no matter how far I went.

The dark witch would beat me, swallow me whole.

15 years old, who am I?

The air that is neither winter nor spring filled my lungs.

The pansies, the tulips, the crocuses, rebirthing.

My tree, life sprouting from its fingertips.

I check in on my tree family.

How is baby Fay? I recall her body was not faring well last year.

A voice whispers in my ear: look up.

My tree has an intruder, a rope caught up in its limbs.

Even in the strongest gale, it would not give.

I balance on my tippy toes in my threadbare soul-popping Chuck Taylors.

Extend my eczema-plagued hand and tug the scratchy textile down.

I notice the people staring. But this time,

I don't have a care in the world.

I just untangled my tree, my family, myself.

So this is freedom.

No rhymes, little punctuations an odd mix of metaphor and associations, and a message about freedom that she still found reassuring.

By the time Sally arrived back at the Lansing airport two days later, she had decided to return to her poetry. Noah enthusiastically supported her decision. She was accepted into the MFA poetry program at Michigan State, received her degree three years later, taught an occasional course at Lansing Community College, and was in the midst of reworking what she hoped would be her first published collection of poetry when Noah died. Now, six months later, she hoped that the discipline of going to The Writer's Place, would put her back on course.

It's not that there wasn't enough space in her generous-sized L-shaped studio apartment to write. There was even a small desk that faced out onto Sixth Avenue as well as several comfortable chairs where she could sit with her lap-top or the black and white cardboard school composition notebooks that she favored, along with her Mirado Black Warrior HB2 pencils. But for her, at this point in her life, it was routine that she craved, especially if it brought her out into the world, even if the actual art of writing was a solitary act. There was comfort in knowing that four afternoons a week that 6' by 8' cubicle was hers and hers alone, her private space for her own private thoughts, that one day, she hoped would become public.

Chapter Five

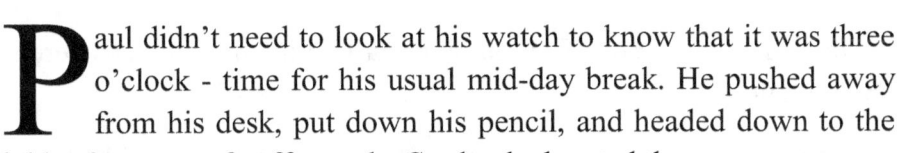

P aul didn't need to look at his watch to know that it was three o'clock - time for his usual mid-day break. He pushed away from his desk, put down his pencil, and headed down to the lobby for a cup of coffee at the Starbucks located there.

Such had been his routine since he first started working at Gotham Graphic Design. It was a small shop that specialized in producing and editing advertisements and publications for a wide variety of commercial clients' small businesses, insurance companies, several non-profits, even a publishing house that specialized in young adult graphic novels.

He enjoyed what he did, especially the occasional opportunity to practice his skills as a cartoonist, something that he pursued for his own pleasure outside of work. Although he did not socialize much with his office-mates, he got along well with Tim Conway and Betsy Margulies, the two other staff artists, and especially with Sam Schneider owner, salesman and chief designer, who had hired him fifteen years ago after he had completed an undergraduate degree at Columbia, majoring in English, followed by a two-year MFA program in Fine Arts at Pratt.

Paul paid for his coffee and sat down at one of the tables situated against a wall of glass that looked out onto the lobby. He opened the small, drawing pad that rarely left his side, took a pencil out of his shirt pocket and began revising a sketch that he had begun the day before.

So buried was he in his work, that, at first, he did not notice Sally standing opposite him. She had spent the better part of two hours working on a poem. Pleased with her progress, she decided to reward herself with some coffee and a muffin. After making her purchases, she discovered that all the chairs were occupied, except one empty seat at Paul's table.

"Excuse me," she said. "Do you mind if I sit down?"

In typical New York fashion, without looking up, Paul answered, "Be my guest."

Sally sat down, peeled off the paper surrounding her blueberry muffin, broke off a piece, took a bite, and sipped her coffee. She opened her notebook that she had brought with her, took out her pencil, and began re-reading her afternoon's work. Silently, she mouthed the words that gave her so much pleasure. At one point, so taken was she with her own creation, she couldn't contain a slight chuckle.

"So sorry," she quickly apologized.

"Not a problem," Paul responded, looking up for the first time since Sally had joined him.

It was her! No doubt about it. This was the very woman he had followed up Eighth Avenue only a few days before!

"Are you alright? I didn't mean to startle you."

"No. I'm fine," Paul said, completely caught off guard in the moment.

"Mirado Black Warrior #2HB, my favorite."

"What's that?" Paul asked.

24

"I see you use the same pencil to draw with that I use for writing," Sally responded, waving her pencil in the air, surprised by her own boldness. But there was something about this man that…

Regaining his composure, Paul asked, "What do you write?"

"Poems. What do you draw?"

"Cartoons."

"About what?"

"Depends. And you?"

"Depends."

"Can I ask?" Paul continued. "What are you working on there?"

Sally blushed. "My imagination, I guess. And tangentially, cows."

"You're kidding. That's what my cartoon is about."

"Your imagination?"

"No. Cows."

"May I see?"

Paul smiled shyly. Sheepishly, he pushed his pad towards her – a sketch of carefully drawn cows, running helter-skelter, with crazed looks on their faces, above a caption that declared UDDER MADDNESS!

Sally burst out laughing. "That's terrific! So funny!"

"Thanks. I hope *The New Yorker* likes it as much as you do."

"Wow. Every poet's dream."

"Overrated and a closed shop, but I keep trying. It's what we do."

"What do you mean?" Sally asked.

"Artists. We keep trying. You draw, you write, you paint, you act, because you have no choice. It's something you have to do. But once in a while, it's nice to be noticed. So, what about your poem?"

"Oh!"

"Fair is fair. Can I read it? Or better still, why don't you read it to me?"

"Here?"

"Sure. It's New York. No one will notice."

Sally laughed. For the second time in five minutes in the company of a total stranger. Her first laughs, she realized, in a long time.

"OK. Here goes." She began to read:

She lies atop my chest

Sleeping.

She nuzzles me.

Her mouth in search of mother's breast.

A calf bereft of udder.

Disappointed, she moves.

Her head bobs inadvertently.

I cradle it.

Sweet sleepiness embraces her.

I will nurture her in my own way.

By my voice, by my stories, by my own

Chest

As it rises and falls.

Such a privilege,

My darling Sally.

Sally finished reading and looked up. Paul sat silently, staring at her. Somewhat embarrassed, she blurted out: "You don't have to say anything, you know."

"No, it's not that." Paul replied. "I love it. What's it called?"

"For Sally On Her First Valentine's Day, By Her Imagined Father."

"Imagined Father?" Paul looked at his watch. "There's so much to unpack in your poem, but I don't have the time right now. I have to get back to work. Maybe we could meet again? Tomorrow?"

"I'd like that," Sally said, gathering up her things as they both headed for the elevators.

"Same time, same place. I'll buy the coffee," Paul said. "The muffin's on me," Sally laughed, yet again.

They rode up in the same car.

"One thing," Paul said, as the elevator approached his floor.

"What's that?"

"Your poem. It doesn't rhyme. According to my mother, if it doesn't rhyme, it's not a poem."

Sally laughed. "What? Your mother is a poet?"

"'Shakespeare rhymed,' she would tell you. 'The sonnets?'"

"Tell your mother that life is not a rhymed couplet." Paul smiled as the door closed behind him. "Maybe someday, you'll get the chance to tell her yourself!"

Chapter Six

Sally continued up in the elevator to her floor and returned to her cubicle. She sat down with every intention of working, arranged her pencils just so, and opened her notebook. All to no avail.

What had just happened? How did she end up flirting with a total stranger over coffee, pencils, and cows? Not just any stranger, but one, from all appearances, somewhat younger than herself? What was she thinking? Had she thought at all? It was all so spontaneous, unplanned, at the moment. Yet, she had to admit, much to her surprise, it felt right.

Her plan to return to New York never included any thoughts of intimacy or romance. It was all about leaving behind the painful reminders of the world she and Noah had created, a world now irrevocably lost. What new worlds she might create, either alone or with someone else, were never part of her conscious calculations. Where her encounter with this young cartoonist with a quick wit and a mother who knew nothing about poetry might lead remained to be seen.

Paul examined what had just happened in a different light. A spontaneous decision to follow an unknown woman uptown had morphed into a chance encounter with her over coffee, poetry, and cartoons. There was now even the promise of a second meeting together.

"Or was it chance?" he thought, as he bent over his drawing table. Whatever impulse had first drawn his attention to this woman...

"Wait a minute," he realized, I don't even know her name, nor, for that matter, does she know mine!" The thought made him chuckle.

"Anything you can share?" Betsy asked.

"No, nothing. Only that I just met a woman downstairs and...Forget it, it's not important."

"Too bad. I could use a laugh."

"Anything wrong?"

"Nothing out of the ordinary. You know."

"Not really. Everybody's ordinary is not the same."

Betsy smiled ruefully. "Of course, you're right. I'm married, two kids, one home sick, the dog is at the vet, Frank is out of town, I forgot to move the car last night to the other side of the street. You don't own a car, have no wife or children, no pets that I know of..."

"I rest my case."

"Of course, there is Pearl. How's she doing?"

"Comes and goes. Some days she seems all there. Other times she disappears into her own world. Thank God for Louise."

"You're lucky to have her. Well, I'd better get back to the board."

"Me too," Paul said. "One thing...."

"Yes?"

"Do you believe in fate?"

"Whoa! A question that calls for more than a casual conversation!"

"All I mean is, do you think things happen by chance or are they somehow preordained?"

"You going 'Catholic' on me?"

"I'm not sure what I mean."

"I rest my case."

"Touché," Paul responded. As they both returned to work. After a few minutes, without looking up from her board, Betsy inquired: "Will you see her again?"

"Who?"

"The woman you just met downstairs."

"How did you know I met a…"

"I saw the two of you."

"Yes."

"When?"

"Tomorrow."

Betsy laughed. "Must be fate."

Chapter Seven

The next day, promptly at 2:45, Sally took the elevator down to the lobby, notebook and pencil in hand. She purchased a blueberry muffin, sat down at the same table she had shared with Paul the day before, cut the muffin in half with a plastic knife she had picked up at the counter, placed each piece on a napkin, and waited for him to appear. She opened her notebook and began working on the poem that she had begun earlier in the day. Every so often she glanced up from the page and gazed out into the lobby.

Precisely at such a moment, Paul surprised her.

"Black or regular?" he asked, approaching her from behind.

"Startled by his presence, Sally turned towards him, a blush on her face. "What?" she asked.

"Coffee. Black or regular?"

"Oh, black is fine."

"That's what I thought," he said, as he sat down in his chair and placed a cup in front of her.

"So?"

"So what?" Sally replied.

"Your poem. Weren't we going to talk about it?"

"Oh, right. I have it here. I was just playing with it."

"Can I hear it again?"

"Sure."

Sally looked down at her notebook and slammed it shut. "Damn it. I brought the wrong book."

Paul gave her a quizzical look.

"You see, I keep a separate notebook for each poem I write drafts, ideas, keywords, phrases. I jot everything down as I work on it. I was so caught up today with the beginnings of a new poem that I forgot to bring down the one we talked about yesterday. I'll run up and get it."

Sally started to stand, but Paul gently reached out his hand and placed it on her arm. "No, that's alright," he smiled. "Maybe if you want, you could show me what you're working on now."

"Well, I don't know. You see…"

Paul took a sip of coffee. "No, I totally understand. Everyone works differently, depending, too, on what they're working on. Most of the time I like to share a work in progress with folks I trust. Helps me think differently about things. Other times I'm more reticent."

"Yes, I know what you mean," Sally responded, even as she remembered how Noah had always been her sounding-board for virtually every thought she put down on paper.

"Did I say something to upset you?"

"No, I'm fine," Sally cleared her throat. "Alright, what the hell. Now, this is just the beginning."

"Does it have a title?"

"For Sally on Her Second Valentine's Day By Her Imagined Father."

"I sense a pattern here," Paul smiled.

"Well, Here goes." Sally began to read:

Lovely Little Sally,

A second Valentine for you.

You don't sleep on stomachs now,

There's so much more to do.

Smasher of block towers

"That's it so far. I'm not quite sure what comes next."

"It rhymes!" Paul chided. They stared at each other for a moment and then both burst out laughing the kind of explosive, nervous noise that sometimes masks what is hard to put into words.

Finally, Paul broke in: "Did you ever know your father?"

"No. I never knew him. He died when I was a baby."

"Looks like we have something else in common besides cows."

"I don't follow."

"I hardly knew my father. My parents divorced when I was three. He died a year later."

"So, your mother, who thinks poems must rhyme, raised you herself."

Paul nodded. "You too?"

"Yes, not far from here. 'Hell's Kitchen,'" Sally replied. "But once I went off to college, I was pretty much on my own. She died a while ago."

"Well, this has been a depressing conversation," Paul chuckled.

"You don't know the half of it."

"There's more to tell?"

"For another time."

"When we have more time," Paul responded, getting up from the table. "We have to stop meeting like this. Maybe I can give you a call?"

"I'd like that," Sally replied. She tore off a piece of paper from her notebook, jotted down her name and phone number and handed it to Paul.

"Sally Martinelli, meet Paul Goodwin," he said, offering his hand. "We'll talk soon. You can count on it."

Chapter Eight

Nothing but fond hope and good intentions sparked Paul's parting words. But it would be longer than either he or Sally anticipated before they would meet again.

Not that he planned it that way. Riding the subway home that day after work, all he could think about was her. He would wait a day, he thought, before giving her a call. Maybe take her out to dinner at the Cornelia Street Café in the West Village, listen to some jazz afterwards in the restaurant's basement club, learn more about each other. While he ran around the park, his mind wandered further into the future -dinners with Louise and his mother at her apartment, the merits of rhyme versus blank verse and who knew what else - Pearl would be thrilled!

Home, stretched, showered, some left-over pasta for dinner, he settled in for an evening of mindless television when the phone rang. It was Louise. "You need to come over right away," she implored. "Something weird is going on. I could use some help."

It was the call Paul had been dreading ever since the first signs appeared six months before. Little, inconsequential things at first - leaving her house keys in the freezer, forgetting to turn off the gas on the stove (not so inconsequential), forgetting who her neighbor was one minute then remembering in the next - Louise always to the rescue. It was she who finally suggested to Paul to have Pearl checked out. A series of doctor's appointments and tests followed. And then the reckoning.

"Ma, remember the doctor we saw a few weeks ago?"

"The one who asked me all those questions?"

"Yes, Dr. Siroca."

"Nice young man. Thin."

"That's right, Pearl," Louise offered. "Now, you listen to what Paul is saying."

Pearl checked her watch. "I'm listening, but I don't have much time. *I Love Lucy* reruns start in ten minutes. I love that show."

"OK, Ma. So, Dr. Siroca called this morning with the results of the tests.

"What tests?"

"The blood work, the CAT scan, the things he asked you to do."

"'Apple, Table, Penny'. I remember. I can also count backwards from 100 by sevens. You want to hear?"

"No, that's alright, honey."

"It's what we expected," said Paul.

"What does that mean?"

"Your brain isn't working like it used to, Pearl."

"Is yours? We're not spring chickens anymore, in case you haven't   noticed."
"It's more than that," Paul interrupted. "How to explain…"

"Try English."

"It's not so easy," Louise added.

"How hard could it be?"

Louise and Paul looked at each other, each reluctant to speak. Finally, Louise spoke up: "You have Alzhemier's, Pearl."

"Alzheimer's?"

"That's what the tests suggest. See, there's this chemical in the brain called Acetylcholine. As it breaks down, it affects your ability to remember things, your behavior, your moods."

"Don't forget the plaque," Louise added.

"What plaque?"

"Something called plaque builds up around your nerves," Paul explained. "It clogs their paths and makes it harder for them to send signals to your brain."

"I floss."

"It's not the same thing, Mom. But the doctor is going to put you on some medication that might help slow down how fast things deteriorate."

Pearl got up from the kitchen table. "More pills! I can't keep track of all the crap I'm already taking."

"I'll help you, Pearl."

"Louise and I are always here for you."

Pearl looked at both her son and her best friend. She smiled, then headed towards the living room.

"Where are you going?" Louise asked.

Pointing to her watch, Pearl replied. "I don't want to be late. *Lucy* starts in two minutes."

Weird? What could Louise possibly mean? Paul pondered the possibilities as he hurried to his mother's apartment. It couldn't be a life-threatening emergency. Louise would have told him that over the phone. Was she running nude through the hallways of the building, up the down staircase, or around the block? Had she choked on a fish bone? It wouldn't be the first time. Swallowed too many of the wrong pills? His mind ran wild. But nothing prepared him for what he found.

Chapter Nine

Paul didn't wait for the elevator. He sprinted up the three flights of stairs and rang the door-bell to his mother's apartment.

"Brace yourself," Louise said, as she opened the door. "She's in the kitchen. But she ain't herself."

"What does that mean?"

"Let me put it this way. She keeps calling me Ethel. God only knows who you'll be."

Paul looked quizzically at Louise then headed towards the kitchen. Even though he had grown up in this apartment, it always amazed him how small the room was. You could literally sit at the kitchen table, and without getting up, turn on the stove or open the refrigerator door.

That's where he found his mother, or what he could see of her; bent over, her head inside the freezer, frantically pulling things off the shelves. She turned around, her arms full of frozen vegetables and unmarked plastic containers, containing who knew what, and placed them on the table.

"It's about time, Fred," she squealed. "What took you so long? There's something wrong with the freezer. Water's dripping everywhere. Hand me that dish towel and hurry it up!"

Ever the obedient son, Paul did as he was told. But what had happened to his mother? Ever since he could remember, she always wore slacks in the house, her long, black hair, increasingly gray over time, invariably in a ponytail, never a touch of make-up on her face. But here she was in what ladies in the 1950s called a house dress, under a pink apron, tied with a bow in the back, lipstick, eye-shadow and red rouge on her face, and her hair tied up in a red turban that made her look like a white Aunt Jemima!

Before he had a chance to question her about her transformation, she was on him again.

"Some super you are! And I thought you were our best friends! Wait until I tell Ricky about this when he gets home from the club. Ethel! Ethel!"

"I'm right here, Lucy. No need to shout."

Pearl burst into tears." I'm sorry, Ethel. I'm just so upset about this water. If it's not one thing, it's another!"

"It's OK, dear. Why don't you lie down for a while. Fred and I will finish cleaning up." And with that, Louise led Pearl into the once dinette, now small bedroom, next to the kitchen, and eased her onto the bed.

"What the hell is going on?" Paul asked, when Louise came back into the kitchen.

"Your guess is as good as mine. One minute we're in the living room watching *Jeopardy* like we do every night. Then your mother gets up during a commercial break, goes into her bedroom, and the next thing I know, she's shouting 'Ethel,' demanding that I come into the kitchen immediately."

"You being Ethel?"

"So, it seems, Fred."

"She's never done anything like this before, has she? I mean pretending that she is someone else."

"You think I wouldn't have told you?"

"Sorry, it's just…I don't remember reading about anything like this in all the Alzheimer's research I did."

"Don't mean that it's not."

"I'll check with Dr. Siroca tomorrow. Meanwhile, if it's OK with you, I'll just sit here awhile, until she wakes up."

"Suit yourself," Louise said, as she began putting back into the freezer all that Pearl had removed.

"She was pretty good."

"Who are you talking about?"

"Mom. Pearl. I mean Lucy."

"Yes, she was," Louise agreed. "Except for one thing."

"What's that?"

"Fred and Ethel Mertz were no bi-racial couple!"

Chapter Ten

After a week's worth of sitting and waiting, blueberry muffins had lost their appeal. Precisely at three on Monday, Tuesday, Wednesday, and now Thursday, Sally sat in Starbucks, waiting for Paul. She wondered why he hadn't called or appeared for his daily mid-day coffee break. She tried not to take it personally. They seemed to have hit it off. She had looked forward to hearing from him. Stupidly, she thought, I should have asked him for his phone number. After all, it wasn't as if they were living in the past, when such forwardness would have been considered improper. Maybe he was sick or had to leave town suddenly. She would hardly be at the top of his list of people to contact. Yet, she did wonder what might explain why she hadn't heard from him.

Still, it had been a productive week. "For Sally on Her Second Valentine's Day By Her Imagined Father" was now complete, at least until the next revision. She opened her notebook and read it over yet again:

Lovely Little Sally,

A second Valentine for you.

You don't sleep on stomachs now,

There's so much more to do.

Smasher of block towers,

Swimmer supreme,

"Esther Williams," they call you,

You float like a queen.

You can eat by yourself and

Drink milk from a cup.

You read books at the table and go

"blup, blip, blup."

You say "Goo Ga"

And I swell when you do.

Sally, lovely Sally,

Do I ever love you!

All this fantasy about a father she never knew and a mother, who, even before her death, offered few details about what she remembered about him. Sally glanced at her watch. It was time to go upstairs, grab her laptop and coat, and head home. As she headed towards the door, her cell-phone rang, something that, for her, was an infrequent occurrence. Perhaps it was…No. The caller ID announced one Gloria Sherman, with what appeared to be a New York area code.

"Hello," Sally answered.

"Hello. Is this Sally Martinelli from The Actors' Friend?"

"This is she." But The Actors' Friend? It had only been a couple of weeks, but already that experience was a distant memory.

"You and I were classmates there for a few weeks. I'm the Black woman who cheered you on when…"

"Oh. Yes. Now I remember. How did you get my number?"

"Horton gave it to me. I told him I'd try to convince you to come back to class."

"I see. Still, he had no right to give you my…Anyway, you're wasting your time. There's no way I'm going back there. You take care now…."

"Wait, a minute. Don't hang up. That's not really why I called." Gloria went on to explain that she thought that in the little bit of time they had spent together in class, two women of a certain age, leaving race aside, might have enough in common to find out more about each other. And so, she wondered, if Sally was free, whether she might like to meet for a drink or a bite to eat that very evening.

"What makes you think we have anything in common?"

"The look on your face when you ran out of the room just as that exercise 'The Funeral Service' was about to begin."

"And you said, 'Death should be so simple.' I remember."

"That was me."

Two hours later, Gloria Sherman and Sally Martinelli found themselves across a table at a little bistro on W.29th Street off of Seventh Avenue, each nursing a glass of house red.

"Are you still taking the class?" Sally asked, taking a sip of her wine.

"No. I bailed out the week after you did."

"The Funeral Service?"

"No, it wasn't that. Actually, I found that surprisingly therapeutic. Horton was just a bit too enthusiastic for my taste."

"Why did you sign up for it in the first place?"

"It's what I do. I mean…"

Gloria went on to explain that she was a professional singer and actress with numerous regional theatre and off-Broadway credits as well as a fair share of featured television roles and appearances in the occasional indie film. She was always taking some kind of class - acting or otherwise - to work on her craft. Witness The Actors' Friend.

"What about you?" Gloria asked.

"Nothing quite so utilitarian," Sally replied. "Thought it might help me cut through some of the isolation I was beginning to feel. You see, I just moved here a few months ago. I didn't know anyone, so…"

"You've got to be kidding!"

"That I didn't know anyone?"

"No. That you're new to New York. I clearly detect a distinct trace of a New York accent. You didn't pick that up in a few months."

"I plead guilty," Sally admitted. And whether it was the wine or her simple need to reach out, she went on to explain her New York roots, college at Barnard, and her life with Noah that eventually had brought them to Michigan. "Noah died six months ago. A bike accident. I just felt it was time for a change," she finished. Sally sat back in her chair, astonished at how easily she had shared her history and her tragedy with this total stranger who had tracked her down after a brief encounter in an improv class where she had no business being in the first place!

"So that explains your reaction to 'The Funeral Service.'"

Sally nodded. "That reminds me. What did you mean when you said, 'Death should only be so simple?'"

"That calls for another glass of wine," Gloria responded. "If you have the time."

"Time is all I seem to have."

Chapter Eleven

G loria's explanation began simply enough. "Wouldn't it be something," she said to Sally, "if it were possible for the dead to rise up from the grave and offer their own take on some critical event in their lives?"

"It would make the evening news!"

"No, I'm serious. I mean what a relief it would be for someone alive, trying to deal with their loss."

"I guess so," said Sally. "Is that what you meant when you found 'The Funeral Service' therapeutic?"

"Yes, at least in that moment."

"I'm not sure I'm following you."

"Let me explain."

And for the next twenty minutes, Sally sat mesmerized while Gloria unfolded a family history far removed from her own experience, even though both women had grown up in the same city at the same time, but in two different boroughs and in two different worlds. Hell's Kitchen may have been no picnic for a young, white girl growing up with a widowed mother, but it was far removed from the violent world of the South Bronx where Gloria spent her youth.

"You ever hear of Fort Apache?" Gloria began.

"I remember the movie. About police corruption, crime, gangs in the South Bronx. Fort Apache was the name they gave to the police precinct, right? Paul Newman was in it."

"That's where I lived when I was a kid. Three blocks south on Simpson Avenue. In 'The Projects' - me, my older brother and my mother and father in a one-bedroom apartment. City-run and maintained, but what they maintained was never clear. Half the time you could never count on the heat or hot water. Elevators broke all the time. The hallways were filthy. Stunk of urine. Something went wrong with the plumbing or the electricity, it could be weeks before anyone would come around to take a look. One real bedroom and a dinette where my brother slept. I ended up on the couch in the living room until my father disappeared. After that, I shared my mother's bed."

"Disappeared?" Sally asked.

"When I was seven or eight. He was a junkie. Always looking for a fix. Never held a steady job, always on the make. Anyway, one night he just never came home. My mom didn't even report it to the police. She was glad to be rid of him."

"So, your mother raised you and your brother by herself?"

"As best she could. Five days a week she traipsed to Manhattan or Brooklyn to clean houses for white folks. Barely enough to put food on the table and pay the bills. My brother tried to help out. Worked at a super-market after school until he got caught up in a gang. Went off, in his own way, petty theft, dealing drugs, until…" Gloria paused on the verge of tears.

"There's no need to go…"

"No, I need to," Gloria said. "Until he was killed in a turf war between gang war over burnt-out blocks of storefronts and tenements, fires set by landlords looking to cash in their insurance policies! What a fucking waste!"

"And your mother?"

"Devastated her. But she went on. Her church kept her going. And me, I guess. That's where I first sang in public, in the choir, every Sunday. She was so proud. Made sure I did my schoolwork, insisted that I audition for Music and Art High School. Remember the movie *Fame*? That was me."

"Is she still alive?"

"No. She passed in 1977. A heart attack. Two weeks before, we stood on Charlotte Street to see President Carter. He toured the neighborhood in his cream-colored limo. I'll never forget. Surveying the rubble and the burnt-out buildings. Vowed to make things better. Never happened. Anyway, that's my story. Full of woulda, coulda, shouldas," Gloria laughed. "I could play 'The Funeral Service' for days on end."

Sally smiled ruefully. "Believe me, I know what you mean." She then proceeded to fill in more of the details of her life with Noah, his death, her decision to return to New York to begin again, and the emptiness that at times, still engulfed her.

"So, I was right," Gloria offered when Sally finished. "We do share a lot in common. I knew it."

"Are you as hungry as I am?" Sally asked.

"Starving."

"Yet more evidence of our commonality," Sally laughed.

"Spoken like a poet!"

"When the opportunity is there! Let's order."

Chapter Twelve

Sally woke up the next morning at 8:30, an hour later than usual, with her first hangover since her undergraduate days. At least it was Friday, with no fixed schedule. It was her day to clean, run errands, and maybe take in a film in the late afternoon at The Angelika if there was something worth seeing. "Good thing," she thought. "I can barely hold a cup of coffee with two hands, let alone manage a pencil with one!"

Still, she had to admit, her evening with Gloria Sherman had been exhilarating. Not only because of the details of their conversation, but because of the intimate and deep emotions they had shared. She couldn't recall the last time she had bonded together with another woman. Certainly not since Noah's death. And not very often before then. She opened up her second Valentine's poem notebook, where she had jotted down Gloria's phone number before they parted ways. "At least I didn't make that mistake again," she thought, as she headed towards the bathroom.

As it turned out, it was a mistake with no enduring cost. Just as she was about to step out of her apartment, her phone rang. It was Paul. He apologized for letting a week go by without calling her. He proposed they meet at the usual place at three so he could explain himself. When Sally explained that Friday was the one day she was not at The Writer's Place, he offered to take her out to an early dinner in the West Village - even though he realized, as the words left his mouth, that he would be sacrificing his daily run.

And so it was that at 6 P.M. that evening, Sally and Paul found themselves sitting across from each other at a small, paper-covered table at Pesce and Pasta, a popular, neighborhood Italian bistro at the intersection of Bleecker and Cornelia Streets that specialized in fresh fish prepared any way you preferred.

Before Sally even had a chance to look at the menu, Paul began to explain why it had taken him a week to get back in touch with her. "That wasn't my plan," he offered.

"Sounds intriguing. I didn't know you had a plan!"

"No. I only meant that I hoped to call you sooner, but family business intervened."

"I hope everything is OK."

"That remains to be seen. It's about my mother."

Paul then recounted the clear signs of Pearl's mental deterioration over the past six months, climaxing in the strange happenings of the past week, including her transformation into Lucy Ricardo, his conversation with her doctor, and the vigil he had kept at her apartment so that he could monitor the situation and help out Louise if need be.

"Louise?" Sally inquired.

Sally nodded after Paul explained about Louise and how important she was to both himself and his mother. "Sounds like it's fortunate that they have each other."

"It's a special bond," Paul acknowledged.

"I know a little bit about Alzheimer's and dementia. But I don't remember anything like what you're describing. What did the doctor say?"

"Doctor Siroca has never seen such behavior in his practice, but he's read about similar experiences. It even has a name: imaginative role-playing. How do you know about this stuff? Does someone in your family have Alzheimer's?"

"No, it's just that... You see, I was married to a neurologist. He occasionally saw older patients who showed signs of the disease."

"Oh, I had no idea." But before Paul had a chance to ask more about Sally's situation, she turned the conversation back to Pearl.

"Did it happen again?"

"What?"

"Your mother. Did she become Lucy again."

"Just once. Yesterday. Dressed in her Lucy clothes, she came out of her bedroom and insisted that I was Ricky."

"Ricky Ricardo? Her husband, the Cuban bandleader?"

"Can't you see the resemblance? Anyway, I did my best imitation. The doctor said to humor her. She demanded that we sing and dance to her favorite tune, *Besame Mucho.* Do you know it?" Paul hummed a few bars. "When we finished, she insisted that she heard Little Ricky crying in the bedroom. She left to take care of him. Five minutes later she came back out as Pearl, clothes changed, her old self, wondering what I was doing in her apartment in the middle of the morning when I should be at work."

"What does the future hold?"

"Who knows? There's no sure path except that over time, things only get worse. Even before this week, I had already begun to inquire about assisted-living places that cater to people with dementia and Alzheimer's, figuring that at some point, neither myself nor Louise will be able to take care of her. But when and if that will be is anybody's guess."

"I'd love to meet Pearl."

Paul smiled. "She'd be thrilled, I assure you. But I should warn you that even the prospect of such a meeting would make her mind run wild. You see, long ago, she gave up any hope that I might become involved with a woman or ever get married, which is her fondest dream. God knows what she would think or do if she met you."

"Is that your intent," Sally asked. "To get involved?"

"I certainly want to hear more of your poems."

"Those I am happy to share. What else I'm ready for, at this point in my life, remains unsettled."

"What is 'this point,' if I may ask?"

And then, just as she had with Gloria the evening before, Sally explained how she had ended up in New York after an absence of twenty years, about her life with Noah and his death, and about her struggle to begin again.

"You're a brave person to embark on such a journey alone."

"That's what Noah would have wanted."

"And you? What do you want?"

"I want to order dinner! I missed my three o'clock blueberry muffin! I'm famished."

Paul laughed. "In my mother's native tongue, that would be 'famisht.' Yiddish for a little mixed up."

"That's what I get when I'm hungry. And don't forget. I may be Italian, but I grew up in New York. I know what it means."

"My mother would get a kick out of you."

Sally smiled. "I hope we find out soon enough."

Chapter Thirteen

Three weeks had gone by, and Lucy had yet to reappear. Pearl resumed her morning constitutionals down Ocean Avenue to Avenue U, past St. Edmonds Church on the corner of Avenue T, and past Patio Gardens, the so-called "old age home" right next to it. She would pick up a copy of the *Times* and, if need be, a quart of milk or a few bananas on the avenue. Paul still appeared at his weekly Friday dinners. He never mentioned Sally.

On this particular morning, as she entered the kitchen back from her walk, Pearl announced to Louise that spring was in the air. "The crocuses are coming up, and the forsythias are beginning to bud."

Louise put the milk in the refrigerator and poured Pearl a cup of coffee. Pearl took her usual place at the kitchen table. "Remember Abe Schwartz?" Pearl asked. "Used to live in the building on the sixth floor?"

"Sure, I do," Louise answered, as she went back to washing their breakfast dishes. "He moved out a few years ago into that home down the block."

Pearl began looking at the paper. First, she read the front page, then turned to the editorial page at the back of the front section and worked her way forward. "I saw him today. He was sitting outside, all bundled up, with his daughter, I think. And a bunch of other residents. I said hello, but he didn't know who I was. Is everyone there sick?"

"No," Louise said. "Some folks live there because they're alone and need company."

"But Abe?"

"Abe is sick, yes."

"What I have?"

Louise wiped her hands on a dishcloth and sat down opposite Pearl. "Yes, Pearl."

"I'm scared."

"I know. Me too."

"I'm not going to get better, am I?"

"No."

"How long before I become…"

"You know what Dr. Siroca said. There's no clear…"

"Who?"

"Dr. Siroca? Remember the tests you took? The cat scan, counting backwards by seven from 100, the…"

"Oh." Pearl took a sip of her coffee and returned to the paper.

"I don't want to end up like Abe. Or worse. Totally useless, living a life I don't want, a burden for everyone - someone cleaning up my shit, putting food in my mouth…."

"We don't get to choose what happens to us."

"Why not?"

"The Lord didn't make the world that way!"

"You turning religious on me, after all these years?"

Louise laughed. "Only when the spirit moves me. And don't you even think about such things. Think of Paul. For God's sakes, think of me!"

"That's who I am thinking of."

Louise bent over Pearl and gave her hug. "Oh, Pearl." She kissed her head.

"I feel so helpless," Pearl said.

"I know."

"So, what do we do?"

"Take our walks, get the mail, water the plants, see Paul, watch *Jeopardy*…hold my hand."

"No. I mean…"

"I know what you mean. Pearl, listen to me. Life is like this. My life same, your life same. Any day, life finished. Who knows why? I don't know, you don't know. Only God knows."

Pearl looked at Louise in amazement. "Confucius?"

"Chijioke."

"Who?"

"The woman who braids my hair."

What!"

"It works for me. Not the God part necessarily, but everything else. Just you watch me, Pearl. You chart my every move. Don't take your eyes off me. Be my body double. My second skin. If I'm there, you're there. Alive, with me, in the here and now."

"So, this is it?"

"Pretty much."

"We just do what we do?"

"We just do what we do."

Pearl kissed Louise's hand and went back to her paper, slowly working her way through the national political news and on to the local scene, as she did every morning. Louise moved on to the living room and turned the television on to *The Price is Right*, part of her own daily routine. Suddenly, Pearl called out from the kitchen: "Well, Look at that!"

"Who died today?" Louise shouted back.

"I don't know. I haven't gotten to the obituaries yet. But it says here that Coney Island officially opens in two weeks! I love that place. That's where I met Sam."

"Who's Sam?"

"Who's Sam? Paul's father. But you knew that."

Louise did not know that. She didn't know what to think. In all the years that they had known each other, first as employer and employee, more recently as housemates, Pearl had rarely mentioned her life as a married woman. Louise hadn't started working for her until after Pearl was divorced. Paul grew up in a household devoid of any memories, pictures or artifacts of his father. Whenever he asked his mother about him, she demurred, no matter how insistent he sometimes became. Finally, he gave up. But here Pearl was, out of the blue, talking about someone named Sam. Was she telling the truth? Could her memory be trusted? Or was this yet another *Lucy* moment a new aberration related to her illness?

Pearl came in from the kitchen. "It was at Steeplechase. I was there with my friend, Harriet. We went to Coney Island in the summer at least once a week in and out of the water, lying in the sun, a hot dog at Nathan's, and then if time and money allowed, on to Steeplechase, right next door. That's where I met Sam. We rolled into each other in The Barrel, where you entered the park."

"It's not there."

"What's not there?"

"Steeplechase. It's now a baseball stadium. Nothing left but the Parachute Jump. Just for show. It doesn't work anymore."

"I didn't know that."

"Pearl. Lemme ask you something. How come, after all these years, this is the first time you've told me about Sam?"

"It just came into my head."

"You all here today?"

"Where else would I be?"

"You know what I mean."

Pearl smiled. "I am Pearl Goodwin. I live at 2370 Ocean Avenue, Apartment 4A. I'm almost eighty years old. I had a stroke ten years ago, but I still can hobble around. My social security number is 040-37-6298. I have a beautiful son named Paul. He's coming over for dinner in three days. I live with my dear friend Louise, who sometimes asks me too many…"

Louise smiled. "Just checking, that's all. And that reminds me. Remember. Paul said, he was bringing a friend with him."

"Do we know who it is?"

"A surprise, he said."

"Paulie is not usually one for surprises."

"That's what he said."

Pearl once again buried her head in the paper. "Would you look at that!"

"You finally get to the Obits?"

"Yes, I did."

"OK, tell me the sad news. Who died today?"

Pearl looked up from the paper with a devilish smile on her face. "Nobody I know!"

Chapter Fourteen

"Can I bring something?" Sally asked, when Paul called to invite her to dinner Friday night at his mother's apartment.

"A poem, maybe. Preferably one that rhymes," he suggested. "She'd like that."

Sally smiled as she recalled the conversation. It had been almost three weeks since their dinner in the West Village. Aside from having coffee at 3 P.M. every Monday through Thursday, they had been with each other on two different occasions. At Sally's suggestion, they spent an afternoon at The Cloisters, a New York treasure in Fort Tyron Park, overlooking the Hudson River, close to the George Washington Bridge. They wandered through the stately gardens just coming into bloom, found the exact location where Louise Lasser broke up with Woody Allen in *Bananas*, and went inside the monastery to look at the European medieval art on display. One Sunday, Sally took the F Train into Brooklyn, and met Paul at Dizzy's, a diner on the corner of Eighth Avenue and Ninth Street. After lunch, with Paul as her guide, they roamed the many pathways of Prospect Park. Whenever they were together, they talked about her poems and his cartoons, shared bits and pieces about their lives, and became more comfortable with each other in each passing moment.

One salient fact emerged from their time together. They were both raised by their mothers, with, at best, scant memories of their fathers. In Sally's case, none at all. For Paul, only vague recollections of a man who left home when he was three, to die soon after. Neither of their mothers was intent of reminding their children of the men they had lost. Not out of malice or spite; but out of the need and effort required to raise and nurture them.

Despite Sally's distinctively Italian surname, her mother, Mary, came from stern, Protestant stock. Born and raised in Hell's Kitchen, she graduated high school with a vocational degree in typing and stenography. As the United States ramped up for war in Europe, she found a job in the typing pool at Metropolitan Life. Over the years, she worked her way up to a position of executive secretary to one of the company's regional sales managers. Her husband, Mike, worked as a longshoreman, at the very moment Marlon Brando immortalized them in *On the Waterfront*. Sally was born in 1957, three years after Brando won the Oscar for best actor. One year later, her father died of a massive heart attack while loading cargo on the Brooklyn docks.

As Sally told Paul, her mother was the taciturn, solitary type. "She was out of the house by 8AM, five days a week. Came home from work, shopped, cooked, cleaned, made sure I did my homework, had a beer or two with her unfiltered, Camel cigarettes that eventually killed her, watched television, and went to bed."

"No friends or family? Sounds very austere," Paul had remarked.

"She was a bit of a loner, except when it came to me. My mother was determined that I make something of my life beyond anything she could ever have imagined for herself. We never had much, but she spared nothing when it came to me: clothes, tutoring, violin lessons, whatever she thought I needed, she was there."

"The violin, huh! I started playing the accordion when I was nine. Fearful that the bellows might squeeze off my emerging manhood, I convinced my mother to let me switch to the guitar. I made it up to *Maleguena* but could never master it. One day I went for my weekly lesson and knocked at my teacher's front door. A woman I had never seen before opened it. 'I'm here for my lesson,' I said. 'Didn't anyone call your home? Mr. Steinberg dropped dead of a heart attack last night!' Convinced that my failure to master *Maleguena* was the cause of his death, I quit the guitar on the spot."

"What is it with mothers and musical instruments?" Paul mused, as he told Sally more about the woman she would soon meet. Pearl, she learned, taught English at James Madison High School, a short bus ride down Ocean Avenue from where she and Paul lived. Except on Tuesdays, when Louise came to clean the apartment and make him lunch, she made it home on her lunch hour to feed her son while he was in elementary school. Like Sally's mother, her days were filled with work, shopping, cooking, and caring for her child.

But unlike Mary, Pearl found time for herself. Every two weeks, always on a Tuesday, she met with three other women in the building to play Mahjong. Whenever cheap theatre tickets became available from the teacher's union, she went to Broadway shows, often taking Paul with her. Musicals were her favorite. A life-long Democrat who worshipped FDR, she followed national politics daily in the *New York Times* and revered Drew Pearson and Walter Cronkite. She abhorred Joe McCarthy and 1950s conformity, even as she offered her own son a vision of a more just and equitable world. Fondly, she would tell him about going to Ebbets Field to see Jackie Robinson play baseball - what a marvelous player he was, what he meant to the game, and his impact on the struggle for racial equality - even if the Dodgers did move to Los Angeles ten years before Paul was born.

While Sally spent her childhood summers in one city day camp or another while her mother put in her hours at Met Life, Paul, she discovered, enjoyed a much different experience. From the last day of school through Labor Day, until he was sixteen, he stayed at various, small hotels in the so-called "Jewish Catskills" scattered through Sullivan and Orange counties. At places such as Jaffe's Evergreen Manor and the Kiamesha Lodge and Country Club his mother became "Aunt Pearl," the consummate Arts and Crafts counselor, occupying the children of paying guests while they ate and relaxed under summer skies. For her services, she received room and board for her and her son, a minimal salary, and whatever tips she might earn. "I can't begin to tell you how many lanyards I made over the years," Paul had told Sally. "And now, they've all disappeared."

Perhaps all the ones Paul had made. Rummaging through the bins in Under the Pig, a tiny antique store in the East Village one morning, Sally found an old, frayed, green and yellow one, complete with a metal whistle. She bought it for two dollars, took it home, and carefully wrapped it in tissue paper. Now, she placed it in her purse, along with several of her poems that she had printed out that afternoon. It was 5:30 P.M. Time to head into Brooklyn and dinner with Paul, Louise, and Pearl.

Chapter Fifteen

P earl opened the oven door, pulled out the lower rack, reached in and shook the chicken's leg. With a long fork, she poked at the potatoes and carrots roasting in the bottom of the pan. Thirty minutes more and all would be ready.

"I'm going to change," she announced to Louise, as she headed towards her bedroom.

"Suit yourself, but you look fine."

"Just in case. Maybe you should change too."

Louise stared at Pearl and broke into an exaggerated black, Southern dialect: "Who you think you're talking to, Miss Pearl? Don't you get uppity with me!"

"I'm sorry," Pearl said. "I'm just a little nervous about tonight. Who do you think this surprise is that Paulie mentioned?"

"Time will tell. He should be here by 6:30. Food's in the oven. The table is all set. Go change if you want but what you wear won't make any difference." Unless, Louise thought, you come out dressed as Lucy Ricardo and start calling me Ethel. Pray to God that doesn't happen. Not tonight!

For the truth was that Paul had called Louise the day before to tell her that he was bringing a woman with him to dinner, Sally Martinelli, a bit older than himself, originally from the city, recently returned after quite a few years away, whom he had met by chance a few weeks ago. "Do you think Mom can handle meeting her?"

"You know what?" Louise told him. "She's just about given up hope that you might meet someone and settle down. Maybe the news will keep her more in the present, focused on the here and now. Bring it on. And bring a bottle of wine. We may need a drink before the night is over."

Paul met Sally at the Kings Highway stop on the QB line (the old BMT of his youth), on E. 16th St., on the corner where Dubrow's Cafeteria used to be. Now a Chase Bank, in 1976 his mother took him there to see Jimmy Carter campaign for the Presidency. Sixteen years before that, she had stood in the same spot to cheer on John F. Kennedy in a similar pursuit.

It was a warm, spring evening, the sky not yet dark. Much to their surprise, they greeted each other with a kiss, a soft brush of lips, their first touch of physical intimacy, that caused them both to blush. Paul took Sally's hand, and they began walking towards his mother's apartment.

Every block contained memories of Paul's childhood. They walked by the Avenue R Temple where he had been bar mitzvahed on a hot, June day, dressed in a worsted, woolen gray tweed suit that his mother had bought for him from the sale racks at S. Klein's at Union Square. "It will last a lifetime," she told him when he complained that it itched. They turned down E. 19th Street past Connie Maron's house, this hot, Italian, junior high school bombshell who always wore tight, pink sweaters that accentuated her pointed breasts. How he had lusted after her in vain. Finally, there they were, in front of Richard Hall Apartments, where he had been born and raised a typical, pre-war (WWII, that is) red-brick six story building distinguished by its name and by the four, white faux Roman columns that surrounded the entry.

"Who was Richard Hall?" Sally asked as they walked up the front steps and into the lobby.

"I never thought to ask. Maybe my mother knows."

"I'll only ask her if we run out of things to talk about."

Paul smiled, as the elevator reached the fourth floor. "Not likely to happen. Not with Pearl."

But when he rang the doorbell and his mother opened the door, she, in fact, stood speechless at the sight of her beloved son standing there with an attractive, middle-aged woman clearly "the surprise" he had promised.

"Let them in, Pearl," Louise commanded. "You're blocking the door."

Pearl complied. Paul gave both his mother and Louise a kiss and introduced Sally to them. "So pleased to meet both of you," Sally offered, as she shook their hands. "Paul has told me so much about both of you."

"That's nice, honey," Louise said, as she ushered them into the living room. "I hope it wasn't all bad!"

Before Sally could respond, Pearl, who, by now had regained her composure, chimed in: "What could Paulie say that wouldn't be nice? Such a good boy! But you know...Sally? Right? He's never told us anything about you. Only that he was bringing a surprise to dinner."

Sally gave Paul a quizzical look. "Really? I didn't know that. I hope it's OK."

"Fine. It's fine," Pearl responded, before her son could get a word in edgewise. "Let's all go into the kitchen and eat. You can tell us all about yourself."

Which Sally did, sort of, over the next hour or so. Fortified by the delicious meal Pearl had cooked and the bottle of red wine Paul had brought, Sally told Louise and Pearl how the two of them had met and her love of poetry. She purposely left out anything about her former life with Noah or his death.

"A poet, huh? I love poetry, Pearl told her. "Someday I would love to hear one of yours."

"Actually, I wrote one just for tonight. For you and Louise. May I read it?"

"Please."

Sally reached into her bag, pulled out the poem and began to read:

It's an honor, Pearl, to meet you,

Louise as well, tonight.

What a charming apartment,

The dinner was so fine.

In honor of the occasion

My gift, this little rhyme!

"It's short," Pearl said.

"But sweet. And it rhymes, Mom," Paul butted in.

"Poems don't have to rhyme, Paulie. Do they, Sally?"

"No, Mrs. Goodwin. Most of mine don't."

"Please. Call me Pearl. One question, actually two. How did you know this was a charming apartment and that the dinner would be fine?"

"Poetic license."

Louise laughed. "I don't know about charming, but it sure is cheap. How much was the rent when you moved in here?"

"Sixty dollars a month, heat included," Pearl replied. "Never a rent increase until I demanded a new refrigerator, the kind with its own separate, self-defrost freezer."

"Which she defrosts anyway, just to make sure," Louise added.

"Anyways, the rent went up $6.00 a month. Hasn't budged since."

"Unbelievable," Sally marveled.

"Believe it. You have another poem we could hear?" Louise asked.

"I did bring one other."

But before Sally could take it out, Paul intruded. "Listen, we've got to go pretty soon. What if Sally leaves the poem with you and next time you can chat about it. Right now, coffee and cake sounds good to me. If that's OK with Sally."

"Sure," Sally responded, as she handed the poem to Louise.

"Cake it is then," announced Pearl, placing a double-layered, chocolate cake with dark chocolate icing on the table. "It's not Ebinger's, but it will have to do."

"Ebinger's?" Sally asked.

"Didn't you say you grew up in New York?" Louise asked.

"Yes. But I never heard of Ebinger's."

"That's because it was strictly Brooklyn," Pearl interjected. "It was the bakery where we always bought dessert."

Paul chuckled. "Meat and cake were our two basic food groups. You knew what day it was by the meat we had for dinner and the cake we had for dessert. Huge quantities of meat - meatballs, pot roast, veal, roast beef, and of course, roast chicken on Fridays. And always cake from Ebinger's! Chocolate Black-out cake like this, Hard Icing, Seven Layer, and even the occasional pie. Huckleberry Crumb was my favorite."

"I couldn't wait to come work here on Tuesdays," Louise added. "There were always great leftovers and a care package to take home."

"Do you still eat that way?" Sally wondered.

"Only on special occasions, honey," Louise responded.

"Speaking of special occasions," Pearl blurted out, "guess where Louise and I are going in a few weeks?"

"No idea, Mom."

"Coney Island!"

"Are you sure you are up for it?"

"What's not to be up for Paulie? It will be good for my soul. Besides, I haven't had a good French fry in years." Turning towards Sally, Pearl asked: "When was the last time you were there, dear?"

"Not since college, I guess."

"Come with Louise and me. We'll go during the week when it won't be so crowded. Just us girls. Paulie will be at work."

"Well, I don't know. I have to think…"

"What's there to think about? We'll eat, we'll walk, we'll talk. Get to know each other better. See the Russians. Maybe even go on a ride!"

Sally looked towards Paul for some sort of cue, but none was forthcoming.

"Sure, why not!"

"Good. Then it's settled. We'll figure out the details. I'll tell Paulie, and he can tell you." With that, Pearl got up from the table and began wrapping up the remains of the cake for Paul to take with him. When they were ready to leave, she handed him the box, pecked him on the cheek and gave Sally a big hug. So did Louise.

"You were the best surprise I've had in years," Pearl whispered in Sally's ear, as she and Paul left the apartment.

Sally waved goodbye. "Until we see each other again!"

"Under the boardwalk, down by the sea!" Louise sang in her deep voice.

They all laughed as they went their separate ways. Pearl and Louise back into their apartment, Paul and Sally back to the subway.

Chapter Sixteen

They barely spoke as they walked, each absorbed in making sense of the evening. Finally, as they stood on the subway platform, Paul asked Sally what his mother had whispered in her ear.

"She said I was the best surprise she'd had in years."

"That's quite a distinction. She obviously liked you."

"And I liked her. Louise too. I kept waiting for Lucy Ricardo to appear, or some other telltale sign of her illness, but nothing happened."

"It's unpredictable but ultimately relentless."

"There's a part of me that wants to know more about her, but..."

"What is it?"

"I don't want you or Pearl to entertain any fantasies about what the future might hold for any of us. From what you've told me, you are likely to have your hands full with her. And as much as I enjoyed myself tonight and our time together over the last few weeks, it's all happening too fast for me. I'm not sure if I'm ready yet for new attachments or adventures."

"Or maybe you're just feeling guilty for allowing yourself to live life again."

"Who are you to tell me what I'm feeling?"

"I didn't mean to upset you. But didn't you tell me that's what your husband would have wanted for you?"

"Leave Noah out of this! You don't know anything about him."

"I'm sorry, I really am. I'm just trying to…Listen. For what it's worth, I don't have any fantasies about the future, only hope."

"Hope for what?"

"Just to continue as we are. For now. Although I've been eating too many blueberry muffins. They are starting to slow me down. This cake will surely do me in."

Sally laughed and took the cake box from Paul. "Let me relieve you of that burden." Then she reached into her bag, pulled out a small, gift-wrapped box, and handed it to him, just as the train pulled into the station.

They boarded the train. Paul unwrapped the package and found the lanyard that Sally had bought him. He smiled, softly tooted the whistle, and put the lanyard around his neck. They stood together until he got off at the 7th Avenue station in Park Slope. Sally continued to Union Square. "Will I see you Monday at three?" Paul had asked, as he left the train.

"Bring me a new cartoon," Sally replied, "and I'll bring you a poem."

By the time Paul and Sally parted ways, Pearl and Louise had put away the leftovers, washed the dishes, poured themselves a second cup of coffee, and found themselves in the living room.

"So? What do you think?" Pearl asked.

"I liked her. She's smart, funny, and she seems fond of Paul."

"All true. But there was some sadness about her. I couldn't put my finger on it."

"We all have sadness with us. It just shows itself in different ways."

"You think she's too old for Paulie?"

"Too old for what? After all these years of hoping and praying that he might meet someone, you being picky?"

"I'm just saying that…What's her name again?"

"Sally."

"Sally, right. She said she's a poet?"

"That's right," Louise answered, sensing that Pearl was about to drift somewhere else. "Remember, she left us a poem of hers. You want to read it?"

"You read it."

Louise unfolded the paper Sally had given her and read, out loud, the poem that began with the line "She lies atop my chest," the first poem Sally had shared with Paul.

When she was finished, Pearl asked: "What's it called?"

"For Sally On Her First Valentine's Day, By Her Imagined Father," Louise said, handing the poem to her. Pearl read it over silently several times.

"It doesn't rhyme."

Louise chuckled. "I thought you told Paul that poems don't have to rhyme. What do you think it means?"

"I'm not sure. I have to sleep on it."

"No time like the present. Let's go to bed." With that, Louise took Pearl's cup and headed towards the kitchen.

"You go ahead. I just need to be alone a while. I'll see you in the morning."

After Louise left, Pearl sat still for a few minutes. Then, she got up from her chair, and went to one of the bookcases that bordered the fake fireplace along one of the living room walls. She searched through the shelves until she found the volume she was looking for. Back in her chair, she rifled through it until she came across a folded, single sheet of paper hidden there. By the time she finished reading it, tears were rolling down her face. Then, she put the paper back in the book, and returned it to its proper place.

"What to tell Paulie?" she muttered, as she headed towards her bedroom. "Ricky! Ricky will know!"

Chapter Seventeen

GOSPEL LIKE NEVER BEFORE

GLORIA SHERMAN IN CONCERT

Pangea, 178 2nd Avenue

Thursday – Sunday at 7:30P.M.

April 2 – April 16, 2005

Reservations: 212-433-6709

"Hope you can make it Opening Night!" Gloria wrote in her accompanying email that Sally had been expecting. "It would mean the world to me!"

Gloria's gig was a wonderful surprise. She had told Sally the news the week after they had dinner together. An act scheduled at the popular cabaret club had cancelled. Gloria was called in to audition and booked the job. The salary was less important than the opportunity. A chance to showcase her talent to musical directors and casting offices who, she hoped, might come, and listen to her sing.

And so, two weeks after Pearl, Louise, Paul, and Sally had dinner together in Brooklyn, they found themselves seated at a corner table at Pangea, an intimate East Village bistro not far from Tompkins Square Park, enjoying a prix fixe meal, while they waited for Sally's new friend to take the stage. It had been Paul's idea. And his treat. Ever the thoughtful son, he even paid for the car service to bring his mother and Louise from Brooklyn.

Not without some trepidation. Louise phoned him the day after they had first of all met at the apartment. She told Paul that she had found Pearl that morning, dressed as Lucy, agitated, wandering from room to room, in search of Ricky. "'Ethel, I have to find Ricky. I have to ask him something important,' she says. And before I could stop her, she grabbed her purse and was out the door. By the time I put some clothes on and went downstairs, she was nowhere in sight. I walked towards Avenue U, her usual route in the morning. Nothing. By the time I got back home, I was ready to call the police. And there she was. Sitting at the kitchen table, drinking her coffee, and listening to the radio like nothing had happened. 'Where have you been, Louise?' she says to me. 'I was getting worried.'"

Over the next ten days, Lucy "appeared" several more times, calmer, each instance. The last time it happened, according to Louise, Pearl assured her that "Ricky had told her what to do." Paul consulted Dr. Siroca, who encouraged him to take it one day and one episode at a time. "Try not to overreact to whatever your mother does," he advised, "as long as she does no harm to herself. Treat her as normally as you can. Only time will tell. "When he told the doctor about his mother's plans to go to Coney Island, Siroca approved." The more she lives life, the more life she will have," he responded. If Coney Island was OK, Paul decided, dinner at Pangea was worth the risk.

So far, the evening had gone well. Sally told Pearl and Louise how she had met Gloria. How excited Gloria was that they were all there. After the dinner plates had been cleared and coffee served, Pearl said to Sally: "I read your poem."

"I hope you enjoyed it."

"I did. You know, Paulie never knew his father either."

"I know. He told me. What do you think it means? My poem."

Pearl thought for a moment before she began to speak. "Longing. Loss of course, but also the promise of life and its possibilities."

Sally leaned over and kissed Pearl on the cheek.

"What? You thought I was too old?"

"No!" Sally responded.

"You are never too old. Only if you let yourself be. Don't you forget that. You too, Paulie!"

"I won't, Mom."

"You got any other poems for us to read?" Louise asked.

"I'm working on some. I don't write a poem every day. That's not how it works."

"Why not?" Louise asked.

"The creative process. Finding the inspiration, the moment, the source, the images." Sally sensed she was losing Louise. "It's hard to explain."

"Process, shamsass!" Pearl interjected. "You hear the words. You write them down."

"It's not so easy. No different than when I make a cartoon."

"What could be so hard?" Pearl responded.

"So where are your poems?" Sally asked.

"What?"

"If it's so easy, where are your poems?"

"I have no poems. Women like me. There was never any time to just sit around and write poems."

Pearl's retort hurt Sally. She could see it in her eyes. "I'm sorry," she said. "I didn't mean it the way it sounded."

"How did you mean it?"

"Only that I had my hands full working full-time, raising Paulie, finding some time for myself, trying to be…"

"Cleaning the apartment, the night before I came to clean," Louise offered, attempting to lighten the mood.

"That's too bad," Sally said to Pearl. "Given what little I know of your life, I'm sure you must have had many experiences worthy of poems."

"I don't know about poems," Pearl smiled. "But stories? That's another story!"

Before they could continue their conversation, the lights dimmed in the room, except for a single spotlight. A voice over the loudspeaker system thanked everyone for coming and introduced Gloria Sherman to the house. The Bob Lewis Trio piano, bass, drums and began to play. Dressed in a black sheath dress, a red gardenia in her hair vaguely reminiscent of Lady Day, Gloria strolled through the house and took center stage.

Gloria bowed to the trio then turned to the audience, barely able to contain her excitement. "This evening of what I call 'Gospel Like Never Before,' is dedicated to my mother, Rachel. I first learned these songs singing by her side at the Watkins Baptist Church in the South Bronx, where she took me every Sunday until the day she died. This is for you, Mom."

On cue, the band broke into *Never Would Have It Made*. For the next forty minutes, one song followed after another, occasional patter in between. Many were familiar to the crowd. Occasionally, at Gloria's urging, they joined in clapping in rhythm, humming, even singing a line or two. For the most part, Paul and Sally were silent. Sally remained intent on watching Gloria's every move. Paul kept his focus on Sally. Pearl took it all in, her fingers often tapping on the table in sync with the music.

But Louise! Louise was in her element. She knew the words of every song. By the time Gloria came to the end of her set of *Nobody Knows The Trouble I See* and *Old Man River*, Louise was with her word for word; her voice growing louder by the moment. Pearl nudged her to quiet down. A few people at tables close by shushed her, but Louise carried on.

Toward the end of *Old Man River*, Gloria took notice. "Who's singing contralto to my soprano?" she joked, walking towards Louise as the band continued to play. When she got to her table, she squeezed Sally's shoulder, encouraged Louise to stand, and put the microphone between them.

"What's your name?" she asked.

"Louise Barnett."

"Where did you learn to sing like that?"

"Same place you did, only further south."

The audience laughed. Gloria too.

"Take it home with me, Mama," she said. And together, the two belted out the song's final stanza:

Ah gets weary

An' sick of tryin'

Ah'm tired of livin'

An' scared of dyin'

But ol' man river

He jes keeps rolling along.

When they finished, the room burst into applause. Gloria gave Louise a hug and returned to the stage. She finished the evening by herself with an acapella version of *Amazing Grace* before taking her bows to a standing ovation.

The lights came back on. Some people left. Others ordered another drink or finished their desserts. Gloria made the rounds, stopping by a few tables to talk to some actor friends. Finally, she ended up next to Sally, pulled up an empty chair, and sat down.

"You must be Paul and you must be Pearl," she said. "Sally and Louise, I already know!"

"You were terrific," Sally gushed. "I don't know how you have the courage to perform like that."

"It's in the blood. I have no choice."

Paul nodded in agreement. He handed Gloria a sketch from his notebook. "No caption, but I hope it captures how captivating you were! Sorry for the alliteration."

Gloria looked at the drawing of her in action. "It's wonderful! Thanks so much." She paused for a moment. "Listen, I don't know if you're up for it, but some of my friends are meeting at East Village Social near St. Marks on Second for a nightcap."

"You young folks go ahead," Louise responded. "Pearl and I, we should be heading home. It's almost our bedtime."

"Are you sure it's OK, Mom?"

"We're sure. Just call the car service for us. But, before we go, I want to tell Gloria that she was wonderful. Reminded me of you know who."

"Thanks, Mrs.... I don't know your last name."

"It's Goodwin, the last time I remembered. But you can call me Pearl. You know who I meant?"

"I think so."

"Etta James. That's who. I saw her at the Blue Note. We used to go there all the time."

"You never told me that," Paul exclaimed.

"There's lots I haven't told you. I had a life before you came along." With that, Pearl got up from the table and gathered her belongings.

"One thing before you go," Gloria interrupted. "Louise, it was a pleasure to sing with you. I don't know if you would be interested, but I still go to my mother's church most Sundays, when I can make it. Still singing in the choir. If you'd like to join me sometime, I'd be honored."

"I haven't been to church in ages."

"Doesn't matter. Think about it. Why don't you put my phone number in your cell, just in case."

Louise and Pearl both laughed.

"They don't have cell phones or computers," Paul advised. "You can give it to me. I'll pass it on. Meanwhile, I'll accompany the ladies to the door."

With that, everyone said goodnight to each other. Paul left with his mother and Louise. Gloria went off to change her clothes. Sally sat at the table by herself. She took a last sip of coffee, pulled a notebook out of her bag, thought for a moment, and began making notes. Another poem perhaps, or was it something else that had caught her fancy?

Chapter Eighteen

Gloria clearly was a bad influence on Sally. One nightcap had led to another, and once again, she woke up with a hangover. This time there was one major difference. She was not in her own bed. Paul lay beside her, still asleep, sun creeping through a window that overlooked Prospect Park.

Surprisingly, she felt neither remorse nor recrimination. Only that her longing for the intimacy that had been at the heart of her life with Noah had been sated, at least for the moment. Her protestations to Paul only a few weeks ago, she realized, were less a warning to him than a cautionary message to herself not to pursue too eagerly what she craved. As if doing so would somehow diminish what she and Noah had created.

As she gazed at Paul, who had been so gentle and caring in their love-making, she recognized that the opposite was true. Noah was gone. Forever. But what they had forged together, and her desire to keep it alive, remained.

Sally quietly got out of bed and headed towards the bathroom. By the time she had showered and dressed, Paul was sitting at the kitchen table, putting on his running shoes, as he waited for the coffee to brew.

"Do you run every day?" she asked, as she joined him.

Paul smiled. "Twice as far on the weekends."

"Noah did the same. Cycling, I mean, weather permitting."

"Did you ever join him?"

"Sometimes. But not at his pace. Just leisurely rides around the neighborhood. Usually, we ended up in town for a coffee or some ice cream."

"Sounds nice."

Sally got up and poured coffee for both of them while Paul used the bathroom. When he came out, she said: "Maybe someday, we might try to jog together. If you're willing to go really slow."

"I'll go as slow as you need me to," Paul answered, as he took his cup from Sally's hand.

As Sally sat back down, she kissed Paul lightly on top of his head. "You're a very nice person, Paul Goodwin."

"Not so nice."

"What do you mean?"

"I have a confession to make."

"This sounds serious. Go ahead. I'm listening."

"I stalked you," he said. Then Paul proceeded to tell her how he had followed her up Eighth Avenue the day before they actually met over coffee.

"Let me get this straight," Sally said, when he finished his story. "You followed me for a mile, and then plotted out where I might have gone after you lost me at the elevator, because there was something about me, some 'aura,' you said not sexual but still compelled you to."

"Yes."

"Then what?"

"I was planning to go back to that building every day, maybe by chance you would return."

"And if I had?"

"I hadn't thought that far ahead."

Sally laughed. "I don't know whether to be flattered or terrified."

"Thank God for Starbucks!"

"Amen."

"Speaking of which, your friend Gloria. What a voice! And Louise! I had no idea she could sing."

"People are full of surprises."

"What did you make of my mother's comment that she had a life before I came along?"

"Tantalizing."

"She sounded angry to me."

"She was just tired," Sally said. "It was a long day for her. There's something about Pearl that fascinates me. I wish I knew more of her story."

"You'll get your chance when you go to Coney Island. Keep me posted."

Paul finished his coffee and grabbed his running hat. "Will you be here when I get back?" he asked, as he headed out the door.

"Take your time," Sally smiled. "I've got some work to keep me busy. Maybe later, you can help me pick out a pair of running shoes."

"I'd be honored."

Chapter Nineteen

The weather was not quite what she had hoped for. Two weeks after she had spent her first night with Paul, Sally found herself in Coney Island on a cloudy, cool morning in front of Nathan's Famous at the corner of Stillwell and Surf Avenues, across the street from the Stillwell Avenue subway stop.

Coney Island! At the turn of the century, tens of thousands of people flocked to the world's greatest amusement park every summer. Honeymooners and thrill seekers filled Brighton Beach and its hotels. They crowded into Luna Park, Dreamland, and Steeple Chase. By the time Sally had left New York for points west, the parks were long gone, along with the bustling midways full of every variety of ride, skill game, and confection imaginable. Only the wooden frame Cyclone and the Ferris Wheel remained.

Not much had changed since then. Although the Parachute Jump, now closed, still dominated the landscape, a minor league baseball field had replaced a glowing reminder of Coney's glorious past. Even though Coney had officially opened the week before, on this Thursday morning the few rides and arcade games that remained, were mostly shuttered. The streets deserted.

Still, Sally looked forward to the outing, although she did not know what to expect. She knew from Paul that Pearl had experienced an uneven few weeks. For the most part, she followed her usual routines. There had been no "accidents," no lost keys, gas burners left to linger, that sort of thing - and only two brief appearances of Lucy Ricardo, patiently waiting for Ricky to come home from the Club Babaloo.

On the other hand, a new persona had surfaced. One day, after her nap, Louise reported that Pearl burst out of her bedroom dressed to the nines, stood in front of the kitchen table, and broke into song:

We welcome you to Homowack,

We're mighty glad you're here.

We'll set the air reverberating with a mighty cheer.

We'll sing you in, we'll sing you out,

For you, we'll raise a mighty shout!

Hail, Hail, the gang's all here,

And you're welcome to Homowack!

Then, Louise continued, "She welcomed the house to a special night of entertainment in celebration of the tenth anniversary of Neil Armstrong's walk on the moon. 'To get the ball rolling,' your mother announced, 'have I got a story for you.'"

"You better record this on your phone if you can," Louise had cautioned. "You won't believe your ears."

Paul did, and Sally had copied it verbatim, along with the rest of the tale that Louise relayed. "So, two men of a certain age, Murray and Saul," Pearl began, "meet on the street in Miami Beach. Both are recently widowed. Murray seems quite happy, Saul very sad. 'Didn't you do what I told you to do?' Murray asks. 'I did exactly what you said,' Saul replies. 'And you're still unhappy? What happened?' 'I knocked on her door and she let me in. She was young, blond, and beautiful, wearing next to nothing, just like you said. She smiled, a beautiful smile, and told me to take off all of my clothes and lie down on the bed. I did. 'How would you like it?' she asked. 'How about a poppy seed bagel, lightly toasted, with cream cheese, lox, a piece of onion, and maybe a slice of tomato.' 'No problem,' she says, and proceeds to array my you know what exactly as I requested.' 'What happened next?' Murray asks. 'Did she eat it, like I told you she would?' 'No,' Saul moans, 'it looked so good, I ate it myself.'"

With that, according to Louise, Pearl left as abruptly as she had arrived. Ten minutes later, she came out of the bedroom and made a cup of tea.

"I know you told me that she was 'Aunt Pearl' during the summers, but this?" Sally said.

"Pure fantasy," Paul assured her. "We were at Homowack that summer. But unless I slept through it, nothing like that ever happened." Fact and fiction, memory and reality were more difficult to distinguish with each passing day, he advised her. What this day at Coney Island would reveal, Sally was about to find out.

For there they were. Louise and Pearl, carrying something white in their hands, crossing Surf Avenue like two giddy schoolgirls eager for new adventures.

"Is that what I think it is?" Sally exclaimed, as she hugged both women, careful not to knock over the confections they held in their hands.

"Charlotte Russes, honey! Feast your eyes." Louise handed hers to Sally. "Here's one for you. Pearl and I will share."

"I taught Paulie how to eat one when he was just a baby," Pearl said. "You eat the maraschino cherry first. Then start licking the whipped cream. Push up from the bottom of the cardboard cup until the whipped cream and sponge cake are all gone! We used to get them at the candy store on Avenue U, the Ring Brothers 'Fifteen cents for a taste of Paris,' Harry, the one with the mole on his cheek, used to say. I always told Paulie that the art of eating one was as satisfying as the taste."

"I can't wait," Sally said, as she popped the cherry in the mouth and began to lick the whipped cream. She gagged immediately and spit out the plastic, chemical mixture that passed for it. The sponge cake was no better, hard and stale with the consistency of a hockey puck. "So much for nostalgia," she said, as she deposited the remains in a garbage pail. Once Louise and Pearl stopped laughing, they followed suit.

"Where to first," Sally asked. "It's a little too early for a hot dog and French fries."

Pearl spoke up. "I want to walk on the beach, down by the water. I want to show you the spot where I first met Sam."

"Paul's father?" Sally asked.

"Yes. I told you I met him at Coney Island."

"You told me you met him at Steeple Chase in the Barrel," Louise noted.

"That was after. First, I saw him was in the water. Follow me."

And off Pearl went, down Stillwell Avenue, past Nathan's, hobbling slowly in hot pursuit of her destination. Up the stairs to the boardwalk, a left turn, a few blocks down to West 8th Street near the Aquarium, and then onto the beach and down to the water where a rocky jetty extended a good thirty yards into the ocean.

Pointing to a rock half-way out, she said, "I sat right there. What a strong swimmer. And when he came out of the water! My God! Such a body. My Adonis! So tan, light brown hair, and a smile to match. Right then and there, I knew he would be mine. I followed him to Nathan's. Then to Steeple Chase and the Barrel. The rest is history!"

And then, out of nowhere, Pearl burst into song:

By the sea, by the sea, by the beautiful sea!

You and me, you and me, oh how happy we'll be!

When each wave comes a-rolling in

We will duck or swim,

And we'll float and fool around the water.

Over and under, and then up for air,

Pa is rich, Ma is rich, so now what do we care?

I love to be beside your side, beside the sea,

Beside the seaside, by the beautiful sea!

Louise joined in from "over and under" until the end, and then she and Pearl almost fell down, they were laughing so hard.

"You stalked him!" Sally declared.

"I guess you could say that. I had no choice."

"Like mother, like son," Sally muttered.

"What's that?"

"Nothing."

"This is all way before my time," Louise added. "What year are we talking about?"

"1945. Right after the war. I was twenty," Pearl said.

"Let me see if I have this right," Sally asked. "Paul was born in 1967. So, you and Sam were together for more than twenty years before he came along."

Pearl hesitated. "Something like that."

"What did you both do? Where did you live? When did you get married?"

"Why so many questions?" Pearl asked, as they headed back towards Nathan's.

"I'm not sure," Sally admitted. "I mean, I do think it's important to keep alive the stories of those who came before us."

"I'm not going anywhere just yet," Pearl laughed.

"I didn't mean it that way."

"Well, I can tell you one thing," Louise chimed in. "I never met Sam. I didn't start working for you until you were divorced. Before that, she never told me nothing."

"And that's how it's going to stay," Pearl admonished.

At Nathan's, Pearl found a table while Louise and Sally went to pick up hot dogs, fries, and coffee. "See if they still have chow mien sandwiches," Pearl yelled after them. Alas, that specialty had long since disappeared.

"Did you bring a new poem?" Pearl asked as she sipped her coffee.

"It's been a slow, few weeks for me," Sally answered. "But I'm working at it."

"Keep going, honey," encouraged Louise. "We'd be eager to read them."

Sally smiled. She laid back in the sun, which had made an unexpected appearance. "I have an idea," she offered.

"We're listening," said Louise.

"Pearl, I know you said that you were too busy with life to have the time to write poems. But you also said that you had many stories to tell. What if we met every so often for lunch or coffee? I'll bring a new poem each time, and you share your stories."

"You're persistent, aren't you? I still don't understand why you are so interested in me."

"Let's just say, at least for now, it would be nice to get to know you better. What about it?"

"Let me think on it. Meanwhile, there's one more stop I want to make before we head home. The Carousel. If it still exists, it should be just up Surf Avenue."

Which is where they found it. In all its splendor, just as she remembered it. Beautiful, multi-colored, carved wooden horses, their leather stirrups glistening in the afternoon sun, some stationary, others that moved up and down. Art-deco designed wooden banquettes for those riders who chose to sit. And in the center of it all, the calliope, music softly playing even though the carousel remained still.

"It doesn't seem to be open," Louise said, walking around the back to see if she could find someone.

"Yoo-hoo," yelled Pearl. "Anyone home?"

"Hold your horses, lady. I'm coming." And out from behind the calliope appeared a gruff-looking middle-aged man dressed in grease-covered work clothes, the requisite baseball cap on his head, wrench in hand.

"How much for the three of us?" Sally asked.

"I'm just getting things ready. You'd be my first customers. I'll tell you what. No brass rings today, but for you a special price. It's on the house."

The ladies said thank you. Louise and Pearl sat next to each other in a banquette. Sally chose a blue and white steed that went up and down. The turntable started, "Daisy, Daisy, give me your answer do," started blaring, and around they went, faster and faster with each revolution.

For an instant, Sally was a scared little girl again, out of control, fearful that the ride would never end. "Hang in there, girl," Louise yelled to her over the music, "you look fantastic." And in that moment, Sally realized that she was a free spirit, able to let go and enjoy life as it came to her.

When the ride ended, Sally gave the man a $10.00 tip and a hug to boot. "Until next time," she said. "We'll be back."

"Yes," Pearl concurred. "Little Ricky would love this. I can't wait to tell him about it when he wakes up from his nap."

Louise looked at Sally and then said: "You're so right, Lucy. Let's go home and see him."

With that, Louise and Sally latched arms with Pearl and began walking slowly to the subway. What the future held for the three of them remained to be seen.

Chapter Twenty

The following Sunday morning, Pearl made up her mind. After Louise left early to meet Gloria at her church for the first time, she called the phone number that Sally had given her and told her she was ready to swap stories for poems. On several conditions. They would always meet at Pearl's apartment. Each time they got together, she would bake or cook something special that Paul liked. "If you're going to spend time with my son," she told Sally, "You should know what makes him happy." In exchange, Pearl insisted, Sally was to provide her with a list of questions and topics in advance that she wanted to explore. "It will help jog my memory. Whatever's left of it," she said.

Sally accepted the terms. When she told Paul about the arrangement that evening at his apartment, he laughed. "Brace yourself," he said. "You've already tasted her best. She can roast a chicken, but everything else she touches is barely edible."

"But she insisted that you love her cooking!"

"She's, my mother. I wouldn't hurt her feelings. Just be prepared for overdone food and lots of gas."

Sally laughed.

"Tell me something. What is it you're after, aside from indigestion? What do you want to know about her life?"

Sally thought for a moment. "I've asked myself the same question." She then explained to Paul how difficult the last year had been for her. And how, over the last few months, her life had found a new stability, in no small part to meeting him and his mother. "There's something about her, about women of her generation, that fascinates me. She's very different from my mother. But they shared a common purpose, a tenacity to succeed, an independence in the face of a patriarchal world and a taste for life that I find admirable. I want to know more about it. Who knows? Maybe even memorialize it. Pundits always talk about 'the greatest generation' but almost exclusively in terms of men. I know there's more to the story."

"So, you're giving up poetry for history?"

"There not mutually exclusive. Think of Walt Whitman! And then, there's you."

"Me? I'm no poet."

"Yes. But by talking to your mother about her life, who knows what I might discover about yours!"

"Why do you care?"

Sally gazed at Paul, then kissed him tenderly. "It might come in handy down the road."

"How can you trust what she tells you? Her memory is failing, like everything else. Look at what she told you about my father."

"What do you remember about him?"

"Nothing. I was three when he left. A year later he was dead, or so the story goes."

"And your mother never told you anything about him. About their life together before you were born?"

"Not a word."

"You never asked?"

"From time to time, as I got older. But she made it clear that the subject was off-limits. I respected her position. I felt I owed her that, for all that she sacrificed for me."

"Well," Sally replied. "She may have stories to share about him that may interest you."

"We'll see," Paul said. "Who knows what's still in her head."

Louise greeted Pearl's talk about future meetings with Sally enthusiastically. But she had her own news to share. "I haven't been with that many Black folks in ages," she told her companion, when she returned home that evening. "A little too much God for me, but the singing was fine."

"It is a church," Pearl reminded her.

Louise laughed. "You got me there!"

"Do you think you might go back?"

"Looks like it. I am now an official member of the Watkins Baptist Church All-Female Choir!"

"Good for you. Where were you all day long?"

"Well, after the service, Gloria introduced me to some of the ladies in the choir. They asked me to sing for them and then signed me up. Then, a whole bunch of us went to this Southern barbecue place for lunch. Just like being back home again."

"Does Gloria go to church every Sunday?"

"When she's in town. Speaking of which, she told me she just auditioned for a job in some musical that would take her on the road for five months. Somebody heard her sing that night we saw her and invited her to try out."

"Good for her. Good for everybody. A good day all around, Pearl chirped. And then, she broke into song:

"Yes it's a good day for singin' a song,

And it's a good day for movin' along,

Yes, it's a good day, how could anything go wrong,

And it's a good day for morning and night!"

"Do you know who recorded that?" she asked Louise, who looked on in amazement.

"Search me," she answered. "Even with your voice, it sounds like it could have been Billie or Etta."

"Not even close. Peggy Lee wrote it with her husband, Dave Barbour, who played guitar in Benny Goodman's band. 1946. Whole bunch of other people recorded it: Perry Como, Bing Crosby, even Dean Martin."

"How do you know all this stuff?"

"I don't know. It's just in my head," Pearl answered. "You know who would be great singing this song?"

"No. Who were you thinking?"

"Ricky! When he comes back from the club tonight, I'll suggest it to him. *It's A Good Day* with a Cuban beat! He'll love it."

Chapter Twenty-One

A nd so, it began. The following Sunday. And for some Sundays thereafter, until events took their own turn.

As requested, Sally arrived at Pearl's apartment at 1 P.M. By then, Louise was long gone to the Bronx. She was unusually anxious before she left. "I hardly know these folks," she told Pearl. "And here I am, about to sing for them in public. They even gave me a solo!"

"That's because they think well of you. You'll do fine. Besides, Gloria will be there."

"Today only. She got the job. Friday, she leaves on tour with some show called *Dreamgirls*.

"Good for her!"

"You sure you're going to be OK by yourself?"

"Don't worry about me. Just go and enjoy. Sally will be here at 1. I've got plenty to do. I've got to finish the mandel bread, and I have to get myself ready."

"What's on the table today?"

"I just said. Mandel bread."

"No. I mean, what are you supposed to talk about?"

"Oh. She says she wants to talk about Paul's father."

"He wasn't his father for very long."

"She knows that. She's also curious about the years we spent together before Paulie came along. Go now, you'll be late."

"Don't forget to turn off the oven when you're done," Louise said, as she headed out the door. "I'll be home by five."

After Louise left, Pearl finished preparing her dough, mixed in the sliced almonds, divided the mound in half, and shaped it into two oval loaves just as her mother Lena had taught her. Then she placed them on a baking sheet, set the oven at 375 degrees and put them in. That gave her thirty minutes before she would have to take them out, slice them into pieces, and return them to the oven for another ten minutes until they are browned slightly.

Time enough for her to shower. Or so she thought. As it turned out, a bit too much. By the time Pearl stepped out of the bathroom, the burning smell permeated the apartment. She retrieved the slightly charred loaves from the oven. When they cooled, she sliced them into pieces. And then, like her mother did every morning when she made toast for her breakfast, she scrapped off the blackened crust into the kitchen sink.

The connection made her smile. It had been ages, she realized, since she had thought of her mother. "Little Lena," a squirt of a woman, no more than 4'6" tall, who, nevertheless, claimed to play center on the Girl's H.S. basketball team and had the pictures to prove it.

"Where are all those photographs?" Pearl wondered, as she got dressed. "It would be good for Sally to see pictures. Me too."

Thirty minutes later, Pearl gave up her search for the elusive photos just as Sally rang the downstairs buzzer, her own expectations no less clear than Pearl's.

Despite what she had shared with Paul, Sally was still not exactly sure what she was after. She had done the math based on what Paul had told her. Pearl was born in 1927. Too young to be a "Rosie the Riveter," she was no more than eighteen when she met her future husband. Paul was born in 1967. She had some sense of Pearl's life in subsequent years, school teacher, summers as "Aunt Pearl," Broadway shows, and Mahjong, and always her son, eventually a stroke and then the last decade with Louise by her side. But what about the twenty-odd years when it was just her and Sam? What was her life like? Why did her marriage end? How did Pearl, and women like her, persevere on their own at a time when a woman's place and power faced formidable resistance, resistance that still remained? Despite her recent personal tragedy, she realized that her own privileged life was a direct beneficiary of that perseverance, whether or not women like Pearl or her own mother realized the importance of their contributions. All this was in the back of Sally's mind when she sat down with Pearl over coffee and mandel bread at the kitchen table.

"Sorry, it's a little well done. But this is the mandel bread that I always make for Paulie."

"Sort of like biscotti," Sally said, as she bit into a piece. Or at least tried to.

"Dunk it in the coffee," Pearl suggested, "like this." And for a minute, the two women proceeded to dip and nibble before Pearl broke the silence.

"Did you bring me a poem?"

"I did." Sally handed her a piece of paper. "It's called" For Sally On Her Second Valentine's Day By Her Imagined Father."

"Would you mind reading it to me?"

Sally complied. Pearl listened intently, following along on the paper.

"I remember Esther Williams. She was a beauty," Pearl said.

"I've only seen the movies."

"Are you a swimmer, or is that just your imagination at work?" Pearl asked.

"I'm a good swimmer. I was even on the synchronized swimming team in college."

"Sam was a good swimmer." Pearl paused for a moment as she glanced over the poem. "There's more here too. Let it sit with me, and we can talk more about it next time. Meanwhile, I will begin to tell you, my stories."

"Agreed."

"About me and Paul's father."

"If that's OK with you."

"As best as I can remember, in no particular order, I will proceed. Interrupt whenever you want."

"Do you mind if I record you?" Sally asked.

"Are you going to make me famous?" Pearl laughed.

"Maybe your mandel bread recipe." Sally dipped again and took another bite.

"You eat, I'll talk. Record if you like."

And then, for the next few hours, Pearl regaled Sally with stories from her past. "You already know how I met Sam," she began. "It was 1946. At Coney Island."

Sally nodded. "Did Sam fight in World War Two?"

"Not exactly." Pearl then proceeded to tell her that Sam, a Quaker, had registered as a conscientious objector and refused to fight. Instead, from 1943 until the end of the war, he trained and served as a medic. He was at Normandy on D-Day and ended his service with the U.S. 7th Army's 45th Infantry Division that liberated Dachau.

"And then he came home and found you."

"Or me, him," Pearl reminded Sally. "Let's just say, as the saying goes, it seemed like a match made in heaven. And we made the most of it for as long as we could."

Three months after they met, Pearl moved out of her parent's house and into Sam's apartment. "I was still a student at The Maxwell Training School for Teachers in Brooklyn. Sam was completing his nursing degree at the Bellevue School of Nursing at N.Y.U. – one of only seven men in his class of seventy-five."

Two years later they both graduated and, without their parents' blessings, but surrounded by their closest friends who crowded into the judge's chambers, they were married at City Hall. "I wore white," Pearl gushed, "and Sammy crushed a glass just in case God was watching."

"Can I ask you a question?"

"Anything you want," Pearl said.

"How come you never told Paul any of this?"

"What are you talking?"

"He says he knows nothing about his father. That you wanted it that way."

"Please! Why would I do that?"

Pearl seemed truly hurt by Sally's question. Yet Sally didn't doubt for a moment what Paul had told her. Was this the beginning of yet another bizarre manifestation of Pearl's deterioration?

Sally wasn't sure how to respond. She remembered what Pearl's doctor had told Paul about how to react to whatever his mother did, and so she followed suit.

"No reason. Of course not. I must have misunderstood Paul, please. Go on."

"Go on? I could go on and on. Politics, music, theatre, travel, we did it all. And work, of course. I began teaching high school when I was twenty-three. Sam worked as an ER nurse. We had lots of friends. All types - musicians, doctors, actors, friends from work, you name it."

Pearl kept it up for another hour, filling in the details, before Sally ran out of tape. "Maybe we should stop for today," she finally said. "You've given me so much to think about. Like you with my poem, I need some time to take it all in. Besides, it's almost five. Paul said he would stop by around then."

"A good idea. Louise should be home soon too. Meanwhile, if it's alright with you, I'm going to lie down for a while. I haven't talked this much in years." With that, Pearl got up from the table and went into her bedroom, leaving Sally by herself to begin to sort through all that she had heard.

Most striking, was the revelation that both Sam and Pearl had been involved in radical politics. As Pearl told it, Sam had joined the Communist Party while still an undergraduate at C.C.N.Y. in the late thirties. Although never a member, Pearl too, got involved in party activities after the war picketing, pamphleteering, and the like – foot soldiers in a forlorn cause that became especially problematic once the House Un-American Activities Committee and Senator Joe McCarthy came along.

When Sally tried to press Pearl about those years, she resisted. "I can't remember everything! It was so long ago." Instead, she moved on to other subjects, for example, their love of jazz, the many nights they spent at The Blue Note as well as lesser well-known clubs in Harlem, and of course, their love affair with Coney Island, where they had first met and frequently revisited.

Sally made a few notes to remind herself about what to return to the next time she and Pearl met. How much of what Pearl had told her was fact or fiction, history or memory, remained to be discovered. Paul would be of little help. Perhaps Louise, she mused. Louise, who at that very moment, arrived home.

"You still here, girl?" Louise smiled. "You look as tired as I feel."

"Pearl had quite a lot to say. How was your day?"

"I had a grand time. Gloria sends her regards. She's so excited about going on the road."

"For five months! More power to her. I hope I get to say goodbye before she leaves."

Louise sat down at the kitchen table and eyed the plate of mandel bread. "Burnt is the only way she knows how to make it," she laughed, as she took a piece. "I've gotten used to it this way."

"Louise. When did you start working for Pearl?"

"1970. Paul was just three."

"So, you never knew Sam?"

"No."

"Did she ever talk much about her life with him before Paul was born?"

"Not a word. I always thought that was strange. Why?"

"She just spent several hours telling me about him. I just don't know what to believe."

"Maybe ask Paul."

"No, Paul says that his mother never talked about his father. Would never answer his questions. She, however, insists that she did."

"Well, maybe if you talked to them together, the truth might come out."

"Do you think that would be a good thing to do, given Pearl's condition?"

"Good question. Maybe Paul knows."

"Knows what?" Paul asked, as he entered the apartment and greeted Sally with a gentle kiss.

"Well, look at the two of you!" Louise chortled. Must be something in the air."

"It's Spring," Paul responded. "Now what is it that I might know?"

"It's no big deal," Sally said. "I'll tell you later. What did you do all day?"

"The usual. Went for a long run. Then sat in the park, working on a cartoon."

"Can I see it?"

"It's not quite finished. I'll show you later. Where's Mom?"

"Taking a nap. All that talking tired her out. Me too."

"You ready to go then?" Paul asked.

"Whenever you are."

"No one's going anywhere," Pearl announced, as she entered the kitchen. "I just ordered Chinese food, all of Paulie's favorites. It should be here in ten minutes."

"But Mom…"

"No buts about it. It's Sunday. We always eat Chinese food on Sundays. It's a Jewish tradition. Paulie? Where are your manners? Who is this nice woman you brought with you? Aren't you going to introduce me?"

Chapter Twenty-Two

Which Paul did, somewhat awkwardly, as if the two had never met before. "You look very familiar. How do you know my Paulie?"

Sally started to explain, but she had barely begun before the food arrived. True to her word, Pearl had ordered all of Paul's favorites: moo shu pork, hot and sour soup, potstickers, sweet and sour chicken, white rice, not brown, and spareribs.

The food disappeared quickly with little conversation; each person's appetite fueled by the different ways they had spent the afternoon. Finally, Paul tossed down his fork and declared that he could not eat another bite. "Besides," he said, "I see there's mandel bread for dessert baked just the way I like it."

"I made it for you fresh today," Pearl said, as Sally and Louise both suppressed a laugh.

"What else did you do today, Mom?"

"Me?" Pearl paused. She looked around the table, searching for clues, trying to reconstruct her afternoon. A minute passed. She closed her eyes. Her face turned red with embarrassment. "Oh my, Sally! I'm so sorry. I must have had one of my senior moments."

"It's OK, Pearl," Sally assured her, squeezing her hand.

"Sally and I spent the afternoon talking about you, Paulie."

"Well, not exactly," Sally added. "We spent a lot of time talking about you and Paul's father before there was a Paul."

"Yes, that too. That reminds me. I meant to tell you about the time I made this wonderful Halloween costume for Paul. Remember Louise?"

"I was there at the creation."

"Do you have to, Mom?" Paul implored. "Besides, what does have to do with my father?"

"You'll see," Pearl said, clearly excited about sharing her memory, as best as she could remember it. "Paulie was ten. In 5th grade. There was a contest at school for the best Halloween costume. The afternoon before I came up with this great idea. You were reluctant at first. He didn't want to wear a ruffled white short of mine or the inner lining of my raincoat, but I insisted."

"Or the black, tri-cornered hat that on one side said 'Visit' and on the other side said 'Washington, D.C.'"

"I told him I could fix that, but something was still missing. Then I remembered."

"What?" Sally asked.

"I went to my desk and found an old pair of wire-rimmed glasses that had been Sam's."

"You never told me that before," Paul said.

"So now you know. And there he was. Benjamin Franklin."

"Except for the kite," Louise chimed in. I stayed late that day and helped you make it."

"What happened? Did you win?" Sally asked.

"I'll never forget that day. When I got to school, everyone in my class, including Miss Shelly, my teacher, told me I had the best costume. At 11 o'clock, the entire school went to the gymnasium. We lined up alphabetically, by class and by grade and paraded in front of the judges: one teacher from each of the six grades."

"Roberto, an exchange student from Guatemala, stood in front of me. Who he exchanged with I never knew. One day, sometime in late September, he appeared in our class. He spoke no English. He always had a big smile on his face. He always wore brown pants and a white shirt. Today was no exception, except for a red silk sash tied around his waist and a Mickey Mouse hat on his head with the big ears."

Paul paused here, as if reliving what was to follow was too much to bear, even after all these years.

"Go on, Paulie, finish the story," his mother urged.

"After the parade, the principal, Mr. Bernstein, announced the winners. Davida Zahl won third place for her Chanukah menorah costume. She burst into tears, claiming that she would have won if Miss Shelly had let her light her candles. Too bad for her, I thought. Today was a day for American heroes, not the Maccabees. I was so excited I thought I was going to pee my pants."

"Then, in one breath, Mr. Bernstein announced that I had won second place and that first place went to Roberto! I couldn't believe it! Everyone began singing: 'Let's sing a song of a good neighbor. Let us sing in harmony. Let's sing a song to show we belong to one big happy family!'"

"Not me, I told Miss Shelly, even as she tried to comfort me. She also added that it was important to make Roberto feel at home. 'I'm sure you understand,' she said. I didn't. I just cried. Roberto smiled at me. I didn't smile back."

"Poor Paulie," Sally chuckled. "Scarred for life!"

"I never ate Halloween candy ever again."

"Speaking of eating, does anyone want more dessert? There's still plenty of my mandel bread left."

"No, Mom. That's OK. We really need to be going."

"Don't you have maybe another five more minutes?"

"Why?"

"I just thought it would be nice to tell Sally about the game we used to play. Remember? Name That Musical?"

"Of course, I do."

"I'd love to hear about it," Sally said. "How do you play?"

"It's simple," Pearl began. "You pick a musical and everyone else tries to guess which one it is by the songs you sing from it."

"You start with the most obscure song from the show that you can think of. The more songs it takes for someone to come up with the musical, the more points you get," Paul added.

"I'm not sure I understand," Sally said.

"I'm with you," Louise agreed.

"I'll show you how it goes." And Pearl burst into song: "This is my once a year day, once a year day... I can't remember the rest of the words, but I can hum it a bit." Which she did.

"*Once Upon a Mattress*!" Paul cried out.

"Wrong. Here's another song from the same show. "Hey there, you with the stars in your eyes, love never made a fool of you...."

"I know," Sally interrupted. *South Pacific*!"

"Wrong again. Last chance! 'Seven and ½ cents doesn't mean a hell of a lot, 7 and ½ cents doesn't mean a thing…'"

Paul joined in: "But give it to me every hour, 40 hours every week, that's enough for me to be living like a king…"

Louise gave it a shot: "*The Music Man*!"

Pearl and Paul both laughed and responded together: "No! *The Pajama Game*!"

"You're on a roll, Mom. One more turn, and then we really have to go."

Pearl nodded her head and thought for a moment. "OK, I'm ready. Here goes."

Then, without missing a beat, she burst into song: "Oklahoma! Every night, my honey lamb and I. Sit alone and talk, and watch a hawk making lazy circles in the sky. Oklahoma…"

Everyone nervously glanced at each other. Silence ensued.

Pearl stopped and looked around the table. "What, No guesses? I knew I'd stump you. OK Here's another one: "Poor Jud is dead; a candle lights his head…"

"*Oklahoma*," Sally quietly offered.

"That's it! Your turn, Sally."

"Oh, Mom."

"What? You don't like the game?"

"It's not that. It's just…I've got to take Sally back into the city."

"And it's time we cleaned up and went to bed," Louise added. "It's been a long day."

"I'll call you soon, Pearl," Sally added. "We'll make a date for our next time to meet. I hope it's soon."

"Yes, dear, soon. I will read your poem. And figure out what else to cook for you."

"I can't wait."

"It will be a surprise," Pearl said. "I'm full of surprises!"

Chapter Twenty-Three

This time, Paul did not get off at the 7th Avenue stop in Park Slope. Instead, they took the Q together to Union Square and then walked to Sally's apartment.

Sally gave Paul the nickel tour, and then the two settled down on the sofa. Sally with a glass of red wine and Paul with a cold beer from the six-pack he had bought at the corner bodega.

"So, what have you learned about my family that I know so little about?" Paul began.

"Not counting your Halloween humiliation?"

"My darkest moment."

"We should all be so lucky."

"What did you discover?"

Sally proceeded to recount her afternoon with Pearl. Several times she let the tapes speak for themselves; including the part where Pearl insisted that she had never kept her life with Sam a secret from her son.

"That's simply not true," Paul noted, as Sally turned off the tape.

"And that's the problem for me. I'm not sure when to believe your mother or when not to. How much of what she tells me is actual memory? How much is fantasy? I didn't feel comfortable challenging her."

"You did the right thing. I don't know about my father, but the details about herself ring true. The political stuff, however, is off the wall. As far as I know, my mother has been a staunch Democrat from FDR right through Al Gore. But a fellow traveler in the Communist Party? My guess is she knows more about Harpo Marx than Karl!"

"I wondered what would happen if the three of us sat down together and confronted her with…"

Paul stopped Sally short. "No way. You saw how she was tonight. In and out, one moment to the other. And then those moments when her face loses all affect. As if she's in limbo somewhere where no one can reach her, not even herself."

Sally put her glass down and laid her head on Paul's lap. "I understand," she said. "We'll just have to see how things play out if you think it's alright that I keep talking to her."

"Absolutely. Whatever else is going on inside her head, it was wonderful to see her so engaged."

"OK, Enough of Pearl for one night. Let me see your new cartoon."

Paul kissed Sally on the lips, then got up and retrieved his notebook from his jacket. "It's still in rough form, but this guy on the phone," pointing to his drawing, "is looking out his window at a wintry landscape, snow falling, in Burlington, Vermont. The other guy is calling him from New York. He asks: 'Is Burlington on the same time zone as New York?' The Vermont man replies: 'Yes, I think snow.'"

"I love it," Sally laughed. Then she threw her arms around Paul and pulled him on top of her.

"Are we in the same time zone too?" he asked as he stroked her hair.

"Check back with me when we wake up together tomorrow morning."

Chapter Twenty-Four

O ver the next six weeks, there were more frequent moments when Pearl seemed to disappear into herself. She would sit quietly on the living room sofa or lay still on her bed; eyes open, wide awake, but with a distant look on her face, unresponsive to Louise's occasional entreaties. Lucy Ricardo no longer visited, but as promised, she was still full of surprises.

One morning, as Louise recounted to Paul, she ended up as Trixie Norton, listening to Pearl's Alice Kramden lament about her marriage to Ralph. And one Sunday afternoon, when Sally arrived for what had become their bi-weekly visits to sample Pearl's cooking and recount her past, the Homowack tummler reappeared, regaling Sally with a long story about Herb and Sylvia, a married couple of many years, which ended up with Sylvia stuck on the toilet in the middle of the night with no more than a yarmulke covering her most vital part. When the plumber arrived to assess the situation, he told Herb, "Your wife I can help, but the rabbi, he's a goner."

Paul laughed when Sally reconstructed the scene. But he was more interested in learning what his mother had to share about her own past, which he knew so little about.

Here, Sally's progress was mixed. Her efforts to learn more about Pearl's life with Sam were not successful. But one Sunday, over overstuffed cabbage that gave Sally the gas that Paul had promised, Pearl happily focused on her life as a single mother doing her best to nurture and develop her only child.

"Do you know what the S.P. was?" she asked Sally.

"Yes. I made it. Special Progress. If you got a certain score on an I.Q. test you took in sixth grade, you did seventh through ninth grades in two years instead of three. "

"130. That's the score you needed. I made sure Paulie passed."

"How?"

"From the time he was in first grade until he took the test, I brought home I.Q. tests from school and made him practice with me. He was always smart, but not a very good test taker."

When Sally asked Pearl if she ever felt any remorse or guilt for giving Paul an unfair advantage, she just laughed.

"He ended up with the third highest I.Q. in his school. There's nothing I wouldn't do for him. Here. Have another piece of cabbage. Paulie's favorite."

And so, it went. Anecdote after anecdote. No time now for Sally's poetry. Pearl relentlessly offered the details of her story to Paul's mother, as if she was aware that precious little time remained before she no longer would be able to do so.

Occasionally, Sally encouraged Pearl to talk about the larger world in which her life unfolded, Vietnam, the civil rights movement, the feminist crusade, the so-called Reagan Revolution but no matter the issue, event, or personality, her focus remained on her son. "Not that I wasn't interested or informed," she told Sally. "I read the paper, I watched the news, I spoke to colleagues and friends. But between work, taking care of the house, and making sure that Paulie was OK, I barely had time to breathe. I read Betty Friedan, but her mystique was not mine."

"And that's the point, I think," Sally told Paul one Sunday evening, after another long session with his mother. "What's remarkable to me about her life is how unremarkable it was. Once you came along, her determination and devotion to give you every advantage she could, defined her existence. And she managed that alone, by herself, in a world that offered little encouragement or support for women like her to succeed."

"You make her sound like the second coming of Gloria Steinem."

Sally laughed. "I don't know about that. But lives like Pearl's deserved to be celebrated."

"Warts and all?"

"What do you mean?"

"She could be a tough cookie. Next time you talk to her, see if she remembers how she broke the news to me about Santa Claus."

"What is it with you and holidays?"

"Just ask her. And stay away from her noodle kugel. It's a killer!"

Chapter Twenty-Five

W hich Sally did, about Christmas. Over noodle kugel made with raisins, sour cream and pot cheese that was not half as bad as she had expected. Even if it was a little burnt on top.

"What's this about Christmas? Chanukah, yes, Christmas, no. We were Jewish, for Chrissakes. No tree, no nothing," was Pearl's response when Sally asked her if she and Paul had celebrated the holiday.

"But Paul said something about how you ruined Santa Claus for him."

Pearl thought for a moment or two. And then, in a flash, she announced: "Oh, that boy! Sometimes he can be very melodramatic."

"What do you mean?"

"I remember it like it was yesterday. One early Christmas morning. Paulie was maybe five or six. I come out of the bathroom and there he is in the living room, in his pajamas, staring at an obviously fake fireplace in which stood a fake rubber tree plant."

"What are you doing, I ask? 'Nothing,' he says. I repeat the question. 'I'm waiting for Santa Claus,' he says. 'What! Are you crazy,' I say, 'we're Jewish.'"

"'So, just because we're Jewish doesn't mean that Santa won't come.'"

"'Where did you learn that?' I ask."

"'From the song.' And then he begins to sing: 'You better not shout, you better not cry, you better not pout, I'm telling you why. Santa Claus is coming to town. He knows who has been sleeping, he knows who is awake, he knows who has been bad or good, so be good for goodness' sake. It doesn't say you can't be Jewish. You just have to be good.'"

"'Trust me, you're Jewish. He's not coming,' I tell him."

"But Paulie insists that he will. 'How's he coming,' I ask. 'By sled led by reindeer,' he says. I can't help myself. I burst out laughing and asked if he planned to park in the living room."

"'Don't be silly, Mom,' he says. 'He'll park on the roof and then come down the chimney through the fireplace. That's why I'm waiting here.'"

"'What fireplace? Do you see a chimney? It's all fake,' I insist."

"But Paulie is adamant. 'You'll see,' he tells me."

"'Don't be stupid. Go back to bed. He's not coming!' I yelled at him."

"You called him stupid?"

"It was six o'clock in the morning. I hadn't had my coffee."

"What did he do?"

"He gave me this sad look and went back to bed. P.S. Santa never came."

"That's quite a story! It could be a sketch on *Saturday Night Live*."

"I stopped watching after Gilda Radner left the show. Come. Let me show you the fake fireplace in the living room where Paulie sat."

"That's OK, I can picture it."

"I insist. Come with me. Such a funny boy," Pearl chuckled as she raised Sally out of her kitchen chair and paraded her into the living room.

And there in the middle a wall of white bookcases, three shelves high, stuffed with books, was a fake hearth with the same rubber tree plant that Paul had sat in front of many years ago. "voilà, the extent of all the French I can still remember," Pearl announced, as she sat down on the sofa.

"You're a funny lady, Pearl."

Pearl shrugged her shoulders. "You just happened to catch me on a good day."

"Can I ask you a question?"

"I already told you. Anything you want."

"How aware are you of what's happening to you?"

"You mean the fact that I am clearly losing my connection to reality; that there are large chunks of time where I seem to exist outside of myself in some sort of fog; that things will only get worse, until I won't know who anyone is or who I am; that I will likely end up in some home, unable to take care of myself, until I die, unless something else kills me first? I'm aware."

"I'm sorry. I didn't mean to upset you."

"You didn't. I enjoy your company. No one's ever paid this much attention to me."

"Attention must be paid."

"You know what that's from?"

"What?"

"That line. 'Attention must be paid.' It's from Arthur Miller's *Death of a Salesman.* Do you know the play?"

"Who doesn't, but obviously not as well as you do."

"I used to teach it in school. I think I've seen every American production of it, from the first one with Lee J. Cobb and Mildred Dunnock to the one a few years ago with Brian Dennehy and Elizabeth Franz. Anyway, it's what Linda tells Biff about Willy. Here I'll show you."

Pearl got up, found the dog-eared copy of the play in the bookcase, searched for the appropriate page, and then handed it to Sally.

"Looks like you've read it more than a few times," Sally noted.

"You should see my copy of *The Great Gatsby*! I only keep books and plays that are worth returning to again and again."

"Do you mind if I take a look?"

"Suit yourself," Pearl said. She sat back down on the sofa and began leafing through the play.

"Wow, this is quite a collection. Sinclair Lewis, Proust, Shakespeare, of course. Lots of Roth, Lillian Hellman, Robert Frost, Walt Whitman, a complete set of Dickens…"

"I got those for free. They used to give them out when you went to the movies."

"What's this one?" Sally asked. "*The Left Hand is the Dreamer*, I never heard of it."

"Let me see it," Pearl said.

Sally handed it over and went back to the bookshelves.

Pearl opened the book. A piece of paper fell out onto the floor.

"What's that?" Sally asked.

"Nothing," Pearl responded nervously. "Just some notes I made a long time ago. I really don't remember what this novel is about. Maybe I'll look at it tonight. I'll just put on my night table. Be right back."

Pearl took the book and headed towards her bedroom. She closed the door, sat down on her bed, and read over the paper. When she finished, she burst into tears, burying her head in her pillow so Sally couldn't hear her. "I can't wait any longer," she moaned. "Before it's too late!"

Chapter Twenty-Six

Sometime later that evening, long after Paul had come by and left with Sally and Louise had gone to bed, Pearl unfolded the letter and read it yet again.

Dear Pearl,

It has been more than a few years since we were last in contact, but hardly a day goes by that I don't think of you. I know you have never forgiven me for what I did. Nor am I asking you to do that now. I did what I thought I had to do in order to protect both of us, even if it turned out that it meant losing you. And now I am about to lose you again. This time, forever. I write this letter from a hospital bed in San Francisco. Actually, I am dictating it to a kind aide, as I am too weak to hold a pen. By the time you receive it, I'm likely to be gone. The one sure fact of life that awaits us all.

Despite all that happened between us, I just wanted you to know that you were the best thing that ever happened to me.

Forever, Sam.

February 10, 1965

Pearl placed the letter back in the book. She checked the alarm clock on her night table. It read 10:30 P.M. She went into the kitchen and dialed Paul's number. After several rings, he picked up.

"Hello, is this the Club Babaloo? I need to speak to Ricky Ricardo," she declared.

"Who is…" Paul caught himself. "I'll see if I can find him. Who should I say is calling?"

"Lucy. Lucy Ricardo, his wife. Just tell him it's urgent. I need to see him right away!"

Before Paul could respond, the line went dead.

"What's that all about?" Sally asked.

Paul explained as best as he could, while lacing up his running shoes.

"Do you want me to come with you?"

"No. I better go by myself. I'll call you when I know what's going on."

Forty-five minutes later, Paul arrived at his mother's apartment. Although he had his own set of keys, he decided to ring the doorbell, uncertain as to who he would find on the other side of the door.

It was his mother, in the flesh, but her manner and dress belonged to Lucy. She gave him a big hug and sat him down at the kitchen table.

"Ricky, I'm so glad you're home. I don't know what to do. Here, read it for yourself!"

Paul took the letter from his mother. When he had finished reading, he carefully folded it and handed it back to her. "Where did this come from?"

"It fell out of a book that I was reading in bed. I don't know how it got there."

Suddenly agitated, Pearl got up from the table and opened the refrigerator. "You must be hungry after playing all night. What can I give you?"

126

Before Paul could stop her, she began putting food on the table, a container of left-over kugel, milk, bread, an apple, butter, some grapes. Then she opened a cabinet and grabbed several plates and saucers in a frenzy now.

"What's all the noise about?" Louise demanded, as she entered the kitchen. "Paul! What are you doing here at this time of night?"

"It's only me, Ethel. I'm just getting Ricky something to eat. He just got back from the club…"

Pearl stopped in mid-sentence. She stared first at Louise and then at Paul, before noting the apron around her waist. Her face, only seconds before so animated, suddenly went blank. The plate she was holding clattered to the floor. Instinctively, she bent down and began picking up the broken pieces. But only for a moment. Then she stopped, slowly got back on her feet and sat back down at the table. She began to sob quietly.

Paul reached over and took his mother's hand.

"Paulie, what's happening to me?"

For several minutes, not a word was spoken. Then, quietly, Louise got the dustpan and swept up the broken glass. She squeezed Paul gently on the shoulder and started towards her bedroom.

"No, stay! You need to hear this too. It's time I finally told both of you the truth, before I'm no longer able to do so," Pearl insisted.

From talking to Sally and listening to her tapes, Paul knew something about his mother's life with Sam, who, up until an hour ago, he had always assumed was his father. What he now learned, as the letter indicated and as his mother now told him, was that she and Sam had parted ways long before he was born.

Sometime after Joe McCarthy had been humiliated and destroyed by Joseph Welch, Sam had been called by a legal counsel of the

127

House Un-American Activities Committee and grilled about his involvement in the Communist Party, both when he was in college and after he returned home from the war. The counsel demanded that he "name names" of friends and acquaintances, past and present, and the nature of their involvement in the party cause. If he refused to do so in chambers, then he would be called to testify publicly; with all the potential consequences that went along with it. Consequences carefully laid out by counsel to include public humiliation, loss of employment, and innuendo that he was a homosexual.

According to Pearl's account, she urged Sam to resist. But, in the end, he chose to cooperate. There was no public record of his decision nor of the damage it may have caused for those individuals he named.

But the damage to his relationship with Pearl was devastating. Despite his protestations and explanations, she could never accept his decision to compromise his honor and integrity.

So, Pearl said. Although they struggled to stay in a marriage that had lost all its passion and meaning, by 1960, the burden was too much. After they divorced, Sam headed west. The letter he sent in 1965 was the first time they had been in touch in five years. And, as it turned, out, the last.

The more his mother talked, the more angry and confused Paul got. Why had she kept all this from him until now? Why had she told him that Sam was his father and that he had left the marriage when Paul was three years old? Who was his real father? Where was he now?

Clearly exhausted by her efforts, Pearl stopped talking, his questions still unanswered.

"I know you're tired. But you have to continue! You have to tell me who my real…"

"I don't know, Paulie, I don't know," Pearl moaned. "I never loved another man again like I loved Sam. That's why, in my mind, I gave you him as your father, even though it was a lie. It may be hard for you to imagine, but after he left, I led a wild life. I was never serious with anyone. I slept with numerous men, some even only for a night. The truth is, I don't know who your father is or what happened to him!"

What had begun as Lucy Ricardo's outpouring to her bandleader husband ended as a mother's revelation to her son. As if only by adopting a temporary persona could she finally unburden herself of the deception she had carried on for so many years.

"Why don't you go home now, Paul," Louise suggested. "I'll help get your mother back to bed."

"Paulie? What are you doing here at this hour? Did my noodle kugel bring you back?"

"Yeah, Mom." Paul picked up the leftovers that his mother had taken out of the refrigerator. He kissed her on top of her head. Then he hugged Louise, tears welling up in both of their eyes.

"I got what I came for. I'll call you tomorrow."

After Paul left, Louise helped Pearl up from her chair. "Come on, Pearl, let's go to bed."

"I know why you're crying," Pearl said, as they headed off to her bedroom. "He makes me cry too. Such a good boy! That's my son."

Chapter Twenty-Seven

P aul never mentioned anything about his father to his mother ever again. Nor she to him. He was never certain that she remembered either the letter or what she had told him.

What was certain was that after that night, Pearl clearly became more steady and calm. Her loss of affect and her periods of depression did not disappear. Alzheimer's grip was relentless. But no longer did she find the need to become "other people" to make her way. Alice Kramden had been a one-shot deal. Lucy and Ricky never returned. Nor did the Homowack tummler.

Perhaps the new meds Dr. Siroca prescribed made a difference. But Paul believed that unburdening herself to him about Sam and his unknown father had been the key. It was as if his mother had determined to put her life in order before it would be too late for her to do so.

Sally agreed. She continued to see Pearl every other Sunday; less concerned, now, with filling up tapes and notebooks with stories about her life; happy, simply, to enjoy her company. "It isn't brain surgery," she told Paul one evening. "I share with her what I never did with my own mother."

Occasionally, they discussed the poem that Sally was working on. Pearl continued to tempt her palate with everything from fried kreplach to matzo brie, at best, with mixed success. Most Sundays, if the weather allowed, they walked to Avenue U, licking Mr. Softee cones on the way back to the apartment. Paul would arrive in the late afternoon. So did Louise, back from what had become her regular visits to the Bronx. They all ate Chinese food, always "Paulie's favorites," before he and Sally headed home.

Monday through Thursday, they maintained their routines; seeing each other only at 3 P.M. for a mid-day coffee break, then returning home to their separate apartments in the evening. Sundays, they ended up at Pearl's, Sunday nights, always together at Sally's apartment.

Paul made it increasingly clear that he was ready for more. But Sally insisted on the existing pattern. "I'll let you know when I'm ready," she told him, whenever he brought the subject up.

"Am I doing something wrong? Is that it?"

"No, it has nothing to do with you," she assured him. "I just need to make sure I'm not moving too fast. It's been less than a year since Noah died. So much has happened. I'm still sorting things out."

"When will you be done sorting?"

Sally smiled. "You'll be the first to know."

What Pearl knew was that Sunday, May 29th, was her 80th birthday. In case she might have forgotten, Louise had been reminding her every day all week long. "Remember, Sunday morning, Paul and Sally will pick us up at 9 A.M. We'll be driving to Philadelphia to see Gloria in *Dreamgirls*. Then we'll go out to dinner and celebrate your birthday."

"What are we celebrating? The life I've lived or the fact that I am just that much closer to the end?"

Louise looked at her old friend. "Where do you come up with such thoughts?"

"Disease will do strange things to your mind." And this Pearl truly believed. Each day, she struggled to hold on to her grip on reality even as she felt it slipping away. Would her birthday be any different?

If, as Dr. Siroca suggested, stimulation and activity kept Alzheimer's patients in the here and now, then the day Sally and Paul had planned fit the bill. On the New Jersey Turnpike, their rental car rocked with one Motown sound after another, as they took turns explaining the plot lines of *Dreamgirls* to Pearl and Louise, who cared less about the parallels to the story of The Supremes than with singing along with the CD player. Much to Sally's surprise, they knew every word to every song, alternating between back-up vocals and Diana, herself, as they joined in.

As they wound their way through Philadelphia streets, Paul pointed out the Schuykill River, where once he had rowed for Columbia in a boat race against the University of Pennsylvania. After several wrong turns, they finally arrived at a parking garage, near the Forrest Theatre, a cavernous 1,800 seat showcase on Walnut Street near Rittenhouse Square, where the show awaited them.

Gloria had arranged house seats. For the next two and one-half hours, front row center, Sally, Paul, Pearl, and Louise, watched Gloria sing and dance through a somewhat convoluted plot full of romance and conflict, all driven by knock-offs of "Supreme" songs, that at times brought Black audience members to their feet, swaying and dancing along.

Louise was no exception. "Look at Gloria go," she exclaimed at the intermission. "I knew she could sing, but the girl can dance too." Pearl nodded in agreement, although truth be told, she had nodded off several times during the first act.

Backstage after the final curtain, Gloria greeted her friends and introduced them to other cast members before ushering them into her dressing room. "I can't tell you how much this means to me. Yesterday a busload of Bronx church ladies came, and today you. And on your birthday, Pearl! So special!"

"My pleasure, dear. I can't remember the last time I saw a big musical like this on Broadway. Maybe *Gypsy*. Not the original, with Ethel Merman. I saw that too. But a revival with, what's her name, the lady from the detective TV show…."

"Tyne Daley, Mom."

"Yes, that's it."

"Not like this, I bet," Louise added. When have you ever seen so many Black faces on stage at once?"

"Black or White, what's the difference! I'm just so proud of you," Sally said, as she hugged her friend.

"And I'm so hungry! Come on. Follow me. I made a reservation at a little Italian place around the corner." And off they went.

Over dinner, a three-course, prix-fixed Sunday special with a wide variety of choice and a bottle of chianti included, Gloria and Louise talked about church news, Sally filled Gloria in on her writing progress, Paul smiled a lot, and Pearl sat mostly in silence, aware of what was being said but content to just be in the moment.

When the dinner plates had been cleared, a trio of waiters in white jackets and black bow-ties marched over to the table and placed a large, Italian rum, white iced, birthday cake with the appropriate number of lit candles on it in front of Pearl and broke into appropriate song.

Gloria, Sally, Louise and Paul joined in, as did the restaurant's other patrons. When they were finished, Pearl rose from her chair, gathered herself, closed her eyes for a moment and then proceeded to blow out all the candles in two tries. Over the applause that

133

followed, she shouted, "Let them eat cake!" and instructed one of the waiters to make sure that everyone in the restaurant got a piece.

Walking back to the parking garage, Gloria again thanked everyone for coming. "When will you be back in New York?" Sally asked.

"Not for quite a while. The show has been doing so well that I just signed on to stay with it for another month!"

"That's terrific, Gloria! But we'll miss seeing you."

"Especially me," Louise added. "Will we ever sing together again?"

"You can count on it. Three months isn't that long. It will go by like that," Gloria said, as she snapped her fingers.

As it turned out, not for everyone, and not in the same ways.

Chapter Twenty-Eight

B y the time Paul hit the New Jersey Turnpike, Louise and Pearl were both sound asleep in the backseat. "What do you think your mother wished for when she blew out the candles?" Sally asked.

"I was wondering the same thing."

"Something for herself or something for you?"

"Are those the only two possible choices?"

"No. But maybe the most likely ones."

"I know what I would have wished for if I were her," Paul said. "A peaceful journey for whatever is left of my life."

"That sounds a bit existential for your mother."

"So? What's your guess?"

"Long life and good fortune for my Paulie. May he find happiness with Sally. Such a nice girl!"

Paul laughed softly. "You sound just like her. Is her wish your command?"

"Remains to be seen. Although she was right about the nice girl part."

Paul and Sally bantered back and forth for a while, but by the time they reached the New Brunswick exit, Sally had dozed off. Paul drove the rest of the way in silence; his mind preoccupied with his mother.

Would this be the last birthday she would celebrate? Her day had gone reasonably well. But how much longer before she would be unable to function on her own, even with his and Louise's best efforts? A place had opened up for her at Patio Gardens. She had two weeks to decide before it would go to the next person on the waiting list. Although he had a power of attorney and was her health care proxy, he had no desire to make such a decision on his own. But how capable was she to make decisions about her own future? Even the thought of discussing it with her upset him.

While Paul pondered his predicament, Pearl's mind wandered as well; one dream after another, in no apparent order or connection, and only a fragment of one that she would later recall: By the sea at Coney Island. Off the jetty where she first saw Sam. Now, swimming side by side with him, synchronized together as if in a water ballet; a warm, summer, sun glistening off the gentle waves. She sees their faces – Sam, as she last remembered seeing him; her own, the reflection she saw in the mirror in the morning before she left for Philadelphia to celebrate her 80th birthday! "Sammy, Sammy," she cried out, as the car pulled up in front of her apartment house.

"It's OK, Mom. It's me, Paulie. You must have been dreaming. We're home now."

Sally helped Pearl out of the car. Louise followed, and the three of them made their way towards the building's entrance. "Call me tomorrow, Paulie," Pearl said. "We need to talk."

"Even better, I'll come by after work."

"Sally too, if you can make it, dear."

"Yes, of course, Pearl. I'll be there."

"Good. I'll make something delicious for dinner. Not burnt! I promise."

Louise laughed. "That'll be the day!"

"There's a first time for everything. You'll see."

Chapter Twenty-Nine

The next day, Monday, Paul and Sally left Manhattan together and arrived at 2370 just as Louise removed dinner from the oven. The smell was like nothing Sally had ever experienced, but Paul recognized it immediately.

"Where did you find Milani's 1890 French Dressing? I thought it went the way of Ebinger's."

"I kept a few bottles in the closet for special occasions," Pearl laughed.

"What are you both talking about?" Sally inquired.

"It's a special chicken dish I make." Pearl showed Sally the bottle of salad dressing. "You marinate the chicken overnight in this, then coat it with cornflake crumbs, then you put it in the oven at 350 degrees for an hour."

Pearl placed a chicken breast on each of the four dinner plates on the kitchen table, already laden with bowls of mashed potatoes and steamed broccoli. "Come, let's eat. Then, we'll talk."

Even Louise had to admit that the meal was a triumph for Pearl, baked to perfection and not a burnt crumb in sight. Rather than push her luck, Pearl had bought dessert. Not nearly as good as Ebinger's, but Entenmann's chocolate-covered donuts sufficed.

"I got a letter last Thursday from Patio Gardens," Pearl began.

"Yes, Mom. They emailed me as well."

So, Friday morning, on the way to the avenue, Louise and I took a tour."

"We've been there before."

"I know. I just wanted to make sure."

"Sure, of what?"

"That it is not a place for me."

"No one ever said that it was. We just took a look, so if the time comes…"

"Time is coming, Paulie. It will be here soon. Time is not on my side. But for as long as I am able, as long as I know who you are and as look as I can wipe my own behind, this is where I want to be. Once I lose those things, as they say in Yiddish, 'Faltik.' Take me out and shoot me. Put me away. It won't matter then. Meanwhile, Louise and I will make do until we are no longer able to."

"Joined at the hip, Pearl and me," Louise said.

"I hope you recorded all this, Sally. Who knows if I'll remember what I just said now."

"Not to worry, Pearl. I'll remember every word."

Before Paul could respond to his mother's demands, she continued: "That reminds me of the other reason I wanted to see you both today."

"What's that, Mom?"

"The other night, Louise and I were watching old movies on TCM, and *Harold and Maude* came on, with Ruth Gordon and what's his name?"

"Bud Cort, I think," Sally added.

"Yes, that's him. You know the movie?"

"It's a wonderful film," Sally said.

"Good. Then I don't have to tell you the story. Anyway, watching it the other day, the same age now as Maude is in the film. I was struck by what she says to Harold about life and how to live it. Am I getting too maudlin?"

"Not yet. We'll let you know," Paul smiled.

"OK, so here goes. First, I want to say how thrilled I am that you two have found each other. How it happened, I don't know. But keep at it. As Maude tells Harold… I actually wrote this down."

Pearl pulled a scrap of paper from her shirt pocket and read: "Go love some more. Reach out, take a chance. Get hurt even. But play as well as you can. LIVE. Otherwise, what's the point?"

By the time she finished, Sally was quietly sobbing. In an instant, her life with Noah, his death, all that had happened since until this very moment, flashed before her. She got up from her chair and gave Pearl a big hug. Then, she dashed off to the bathroom.

"Too maudlin?"

Paul chuckled. "Just right."

"Such a nice woman. Don't lose her."

"I don't plan to, Mom. Not if I can help it."

A few minutes later, Sally returned. "Did I miss anything?"

"No, dear," Pearl said. "We were just sorting some things out."

"Me too," Sally said.

"Good for you. We all need to take the time, once in a while, to do that. Which reminds me of one last thing, before I pass out from talking so much."

"Never stopped you in the past," Louise countered.

Pearl gave Louise one of their looks and continued: "If you have the time, Sally, Paulie too, I would like to show you my New York. The one I remember when I was young enough to fully enjoy it."

"I would love that," Sally replied. "As long as there isn't another Charlotte Russe in my future."

"How do you know Charlotte Russe? You couldn't have known her. I went to high school with her."

"No Mom. I think Sally meant…"

"I never liked her. Stuck up little bitch. Thought she was better than everyone else just because she had big tits! Used to flirt with Mr. Rodman, our English teacher."

Pearl closed her eyes, some scene from her past playing in her head that no one else could possibly grasp. Then, as quickly as she had disappeared, she returned. "I must have dozed off for a minute. Such a big day. Take home the extra donuts Paulie."

With that, Pearl got up, kissed her son and Sally on the cheeks, and headed towards her bedroom.

"We'll help you with the dishes Louise," Sally said.

"That's OK You two best head home and get your rest. Who knows what wild journey Pearl is about to take you on."

Chapter Thirty

L ouise turned out to be right. Pearl and Sally began in Brooklyn. Without Paul, who got tied up at work. The Botanical Gardens and the Brooklyn Museum, shoulder to shoulder on Eastern Parkway near Washington Avenue, occupied one full day.

The cherry blossoms were long gone and the blue bells on their last legs, when Sally and Pearl made it to the gardens on a Tuesday morning in June. But the purple wisteria on the trellises in the Osborne Gardens were in full bloom and the Rose Garden abounded in an array of colors. The enormous, ugly, assorted fish that swam in circles in the little lake beside the pavilion in the Japanese Garden that Paul used to feed as a child were still there. So Pearl pointed out to Sally, as they stopped to rest.

"Sam and I used to come here all the time when we were first married. We'd make a day of it. Bring some sandwiches, sit in the Shakespeare Garden it's right over there," Pearl pointed, "and see if we could name the plays in which the various plants and flowers were mentioned. Then we would walk on the Brooklyn Walk of Fame, where there are little bronze plaques buried in the ground, each with the name of a famous person who was born in Brooklyn. I always did better with Shakespeare, but Sammy always knew more people than I did. Come on, I'll show you." And off she went at her own slow pace, with Sally in tow, from one spot to another, each with its own anecdote or fact that Pearl provided.

After a nice lunch at the outdoor café next to the conservatories that housed the Desert Pavilion, the Tropical Landscape, and the Trail of Plants, the twosome made their way past the Lily Pool Terrace and out the Washington Avenue exit, heading down the block towards the Museum. "All I want to see are the mummies," Pearl told Sally. "Paulie loved the mummies!"

Which they did. But, as it turned out, so much more awaited them: two special exhibitions, one called *Monet's London: Artists Reflections of the Thames, 1859-1914*, and another simply called *Basquiat*, that featured some 100 works of the Brooklyn-born and bred artist who had died at the age of 26 of a drug overdose in 1988 after establishing himself as one of the world's most prominent contemporary artists.

Pearl couldn't believe her good fortune. Impressionism, she told Sally, was her favorite period. "We have to go to the Met and see their collection," she said as they wandered through the galleries full of Monet, Whistler, and other artists' depictions of the Thames.

But it was the Basquiat exhibit that overwhelmed her. "I met him more than once, right when he became known. It must have been around 1980. I had an artist friend who introduced us at a party in the East Village. You know he began to paint as a child prodigy here, at the age of six, in a class at the museum. So sad that he died so young."

For a moment, Sally could see that look on Pearl's face as she struggled to balance her past, the present, and her unknown. Then, as was the case most days now, after a flurry of activity, exhaustion set in. It was all Sally could do to help Pearl outside and into a car service to take them back to Pearl's apartment. By the time she dropped her off and headed back towards Park Slope to meet Paul, she was spent as well.

"Did you know that the gardens were planned by the Olmsted Brothers in 1911, and that the museum, of neo-classical design, was begun in 1897 and designed by McKim, Mead, and White? Your mother is a walking encyclopedia," Sally told Paul, over dinner at his apartment. "She literally never stopped talking. 'I'm a teacher, I teach!' she told me more than once today. Almost didactic at times, as if she wanted to make sure I would remember what was important to her legacies of a sort to both herself and to me."

"Or maybe it was her way of feeling grounded in the present. How did she seem?"

"Pretty much herself. There were several times when she just stopped and stood still; her eyes closed, as if she was trying to conjure up some memory buried deep inside. I just waited until she rejoined me, and then we moved on. Speaking of which, this Sunday, she wants the three of us to go to Prospect Park, the zoo and Park Slope. Then next week, Manhattan! Just make sure you wear your running shoes."

"I never leave home without them."

Chapter Thirty-One

O
n Sunday, Louise, left for her usual visit to the Bronx. Once intimidated by the prospect, it had become something she looked forward to every week. So much so that Pearl sometimes jokingly called her "the church lady." Meanwhile, as Pearl had requested, she, Sally, and Paul spent the day wandering through Brooklyn.

For Sally, it was a replay of Tuesday. For Paul, a revelation. They began where Eastern Parkway met Flatbush Avenue, at Grand Army Plaza, across the street from the main branch of the Brooklyn Public Library and the main entrance to Prospect Park.

All designed by Frederick Law Olmsted, along with some help from Calvert Vaux – Eastern Parkway, the country's first urban parkway; the plaza, itself, originally known as Prospect Park Plaza before it was renamed Grand Army in 1926 to celebrate the Union victory and its Civil War veterans, a central traffic hub surrounded by two concentric circles on which eight major streets converged; the arches replete with sculptures by Thomas Eakins and others; and of course the park, itself, as Pearl was quick to point out while her son listened in amazement. "You know," she told Paul and Sally, "Olmsted said he made all his mistakes designing Central Park, and that Prospect was his gem!"

Nor did the library escape her notice, especially the entrance, which contained fifteen gilded figures of famous characters and authors of American literature, everyone from Hester Prynne to

145

Mark Twain. "I used to take my senior classes here. I made them read one book each by four of them. *Moby Dick* counted as two."

The threesome took the B41 bus up Flatbush Avenue and got off at the zoo's entrance near Empire Boulevard. "Actually, since 1993, it's now called the Wildlife Conservation Center," Pearl announced. But Paulie, you remember when it was the Brooklyn Zoo, full of all sorts of animals, including lions and tigers. Now, it's the seals that being people here."

"And the red pandas and the nature trails. It's still a nice place to visit," Paul said.

"That's why we're here!"

As it turned out, precisely in time for the 11:30 A.M. feeding of the seals. Then it was off to walk through the nature preserve paths, feed the ducks, and finally sit down for a brief rest.

"How are you doing, Pearl?" Sally asked. "We can go home if you're getting tired."

"We can always come back another day, Mom."

Pearl smiled. "Easy for you to say. Let's just sit a few minutes. I'm doing fine."

Afterwards, they headed slowly out of the zoo, past the carousel, across the main roadway, through the woods, and then across the Long Meadow. The park was packed with people, young families, sunbathers, skateboarders, runners, bikers, old folks on benches reading and watching, every variety of dogs, kite flyers, you name it. And Pearl did, complete with anecdotes about her own times in the park with Sam and the many visits she made with Paul when he was growing up.

"I'm puzzled by one thing," Paul said, as they rested on a bench in the shade near the Tot Lot, at the Garfield Street entrance. "Why

146

did we come here so often if we lived all the way south on Ocean Avenue?"

"Don't you remember? I had a friend whom I taught with, who lived in Park Slope. Florence Justin. We'd come, play in the park, have lunch on 7th Avenue, make a day of it."

"Are you still in touch with her?" Sally asked.

"Not in years. She used to live in a brownstone on 2nd Street between 7th and 8th avenues. 534, I think."

"It's not far from here," Paul said.

"It's settled then."

"What's settled, Mom?"

"When we leave here, let's walk down 2nd Street and see what's what!"

"You're an adventurous soul," Sally exclaimed.

"Remember what I told you the other day. LIVE. Take chances. What's to lose?"

Very little, as they soon learned. Pearl was right about the address. They found the brownstone and the ground-floor apartment where Florence once lived. But as Paul discovered when he rang the bell, she had moved out five years ago and was now living in Boca Raton.

"Not for me," Pearl said, as they headed down the street towards 7th Avenue.

"Why not?" Sally asked.

"Everyone is the same. Too many old white people all in one place. Wait. You'll see. When you get old and withered like me, the last thing you want around you are people who remind you of yourself."

A box of books, free for the taking, that someone had left on their front stoop, stopped Paul. "Here you go, Mom," handing her a paperback edition of *Jane Eyre*. And for your Sally, *The Collected Poems of Walt Whitman*. And look at this!" Paul held up a hardback copy of a book with a garish white and purple cover. "*The Behavior of State Legislative Parties in the Jacksonian Era, 1829-1844*," he intoned.

"Sounds a bit anal, don't you think?" Sally laughed.

"Holy shit!"

"What is it, Paulie?"

"I went to college with the author. He was in the four seat right in front of me for two years!"

"Small world," Sally said.

"Gets smaller. When this was published, in 1977, he was teaching history at Michigan State University."

Sally grabbed the book out of Paul's hand and read the author's profile on the jacket. "We didn't know him, but we must have overlapped."

"Who is 'we' and what do you mean by 'overlapped?' "Pearl asked.

"It's a long story," Sally said. Let's find a place to have an early supper, and I'll tell you all about it."

Which Sally did at the 2nd Street Café, on the corner of 7th Avenue salad, burger, French fries, and chocolate black-out cake that rivaled Ebinger's, Paul assured her as she enjoyed every last crumb.

When Sally finished telling Pearl about her life in East Lansing, about Noah, and about her decision to return to New York, Pearl smiled. "I knew there was a certain sadness about you when we first met. I don't see that on your face any longer."

"Like everything in life, as you well know, it comes and goes. But you're right. And spending time with you, and, of course, Paul, has made a difference."

"I'm so glad," Pearl said. "And now, I should go home. I will need a week to rest up before next Sunday when we go to Manhattan."

"Next Sunday's July 4th, Mom, the city will be a madhouse. Maybe we should wait another week."

"Nonsense! What better way to celebrate Independence Day than by being independent!"

If only Pearl had made good on her word.

Chapter Thirty-Two

"Your eggs are done. I'm turning off the stove. Remember, I won't be home until late tonight. There's a July 4th church barbecue all day long after services."

"No need to shout, I'm not totally deaf yet," Pearl said, as she entered the kitchen.

"Have a good time with Paul and Sally. Give them a hug for me." And with that, Louise was out the door and on her way.

Pearl carefully drained the pot of hot water and her three hard-boiled eggs into the colander and then ran cold water on them. As they cooled, she got a jar of mayonnaise Hellman's, of course, and two stalks of celery out of the refrigerator. She chopped the celery into very small pieces, placed them in a bowl, added a few tablespoons of mayonnaise, some salt and pepper, and then began to peel the eggs.

"What is she talking about?" Pearl wondered as she chopped the eggs and finished making her salad. "Next week is when I go into the city. Not today. Today I'm swimming with Sam."

Pearl toasted four pieces of whole wheat bread, cut up a tomato, and then made two egg salad sandwiches. She wrapped them in aluminum foil. "Sammy loves my egg salad sandwiches. I hope he remembers to bring the Wise potato chips like he said he would."

Then Pearl changed into her bathing suit, the only one she had, a black, one-piece that went back at least thirty years; put on a pair of slacks and a shirt, packed a beach bag with a towel, the sandwiches, a bottle of water, two peaches, some napkins, and sun-tan lotion. She grabbed a sweater and the bag, put on her sunglasses, took her purse and left the apartment.

It took her a while to get to the subway station at Kings Highway. But she was in no hurry. She knew Sam would be waiting for her at the usual place whenever she arrived.

By the time she got off at the Stillwell Avenue stop, the train was packed with people heading towards the beach. It was a hot, summer morning. Everyone was in a festive mood. So, was she? It had been too long between swims. She could hardly wait.

Pearl followed the crowd to the boardwalk and then made her way to W. 8th Street and entered the beach there. She walked towards the jetty, looking all around for any sign of Sam, surprised that she apparently had arrived for their rendezvous before he had.

When she reached the water's edge, she put down her bags and spread her towel on the sand. She was hardly alone. There were families on either side of her; little children running in and out of the surf, others building sandcastles; their parents maintaining watchful eyes as they drank their beers and read their books in the hot sun.

Pearl took it all in, pleased to be a part of the crowd. She looked out at the ocean. "Definitely some waves," she thought. "Should be fun." And then, out on the horizon, towards the end of the jetty, there was Sam, swimming in the water.

"Sammy, Sammy," she yelled as she got up from her towel and headed into the surf. The incoming waves knocked her down, but she got up and kept going to walking, swimming, stumbling but keeping her eyes on the prize.

151

Before she knew it, she was out past where other swimmers had gone. A life-guard on the beach saw her. He blew his whistle and called her back with his bull-horn. But Pearl was undeterred.

"I'm coming, Sammy, I'm coming," she cried, struggling to stay afloat as she gasped for air and gulped mouthfuls of salt water. "Wait for me!"

By the time the life-guard reached her and brought her back to shore, Pearl was unconscious. CPR was to no avail. Her body and her belongings were taken to Coney Island Avenue Hospital, where she was pronounced dead on arrival.

Paul and Sally arrived at Pearl's at 11 A.M. No one answered when they rang the bell, so they let themselves in with Paul's key.

"Mom, we're here," Paul called out, as they entered. Quickly, they realized that the apartment was empty.

"You called her this morning to remind her, didn't you?" Sally asked.

"Bright and early, at 7:30, right before I went out for my run. She said she would be ready with bells on. Then she reminded me that we were going to the Met, the Strand bookstore, lunch at Velsulka's, she couldn't stop talking."

"Maybe she took a walk to the avenue to pick up a newspaper."

"Let's give her a few minutes. I wish she and Louise had cell phones. If she doesn't show up, we can go look for her. You walk up Ocean to Avenue U and I'll walk up E. 19th Street. We'll meet back downstairs, hopefully with my mother in tow."

By noon they were on their way, and by 12:30 they were both back in front of the building, empty-handed.

"Maybe we missed her. Let's go upstairs," Paul said anxiously. But Pearl was nowhere to be found.

"My worst nightmare is coming true. One day my mother disappears, and I never see her again."

"Let's not jump to conclusions. Maybe she's visiting a neighbor. Who are her friends in the building?"

Before Paul could answer, there was a knock on the door. "See, I told you she'd be back," Sally said. "She must have forgotten her keys."

But when Paul opened the door, there was no Pearl. Only two uniformed New York City policemen, one holding a bag with his mother's belongings. The other inquired if a Pearl Goodwin resided on the premises.

Over the next twenty minutes, Officer Diaz and Sergeant Brown explained what had happened. Eye-witnesses had seen Pearl, first on the beach, and then in the water. One woman was certain that when she first started swimming, she had a smile on her face and was calling out a name, as if she were looking for someone. Within a few minutes, however, the waves got the best of her and pulled her out past the jetty.

"What jetty?" Paul asked, fighting back the tears.

"The one near W. 8th Street," Diaz replied.

"I know it," Sally said. "That's where Pearl told Louise and I she first saw Sam."

Sergeant Brown finished the story: the life-guard's rescue attempt, CPR on the beach and in the ambulance, all unsuccessful. "Your mother was officially pronounced dead at 11:41A.M. Preliminary cause of death listed as accidental drowning."

"So sorry for your loss," he finished. "Here's the bag she left on the beach. If there's anything we can do, don't hesitate to call." With that, he handed Sally his card, and the officers left.

Paul sat silently at the kitchen table while Sally unpacked Pearl's bag. Everything was there, including the two egg salad sandwiches and the two peaches. "Looks like she packed a lunch for two." She opened one of the sandwiches. "Egg salad and tomato on burnt toast."

"Her egg salad was the best," Paul smiled weakly. "Toast was never her strong suit." And then he burst into uncontrollable tears, as Sally tried to console him.

Finally, Paul stopped crying. He remained at the table while Sally brewed some coffee. She took two plates out of the cabinet, unwrapped the sandwiches, placed one on each plate, and poured coffee for both of them.

"I think she made them for herself and Sam," she said, as she sat down next to Paul.

"I had the same thought," Paul acknowledged. "How are you doing?"

"Doing?"

"First Noah and now my mother. That's a lot of death in a short time."

Sally smiled. "As Pearl would say, 'I'm doing.' Noah's death was an unexpected tragedy, your mother's, entirely different. She left us apparently happy. In her mind, as the Pearl she was at her best; escaping the suffering that was surely to descend on her if she had continued to live."

154

A moment passed. "You think she'd want us to eat these sandwiches?" Paul asked.

"I'm sure of it," Sally answered. "Always a provider. Even to the end."

Epilogue

Two weeks after Pearl died, Paul, Sally, and Louise took her ashes to Coney Island. They waited until it was almost dark, the life-guards gone, the beach virtually empty, before heading down to the jetty. Louise and Sally remained on the beach while Paul carried his mother's ashes half-way out on the rocks, before scattering them into the sea.

New York real estate, being what it is, it took Louise over a month before she finally found a one-bedroom apartment in the Bronx not far from Gloria's mother's church and her new friends, who had become an important part of her life. Gloria returned to New York, sang at the church whenever she was free, and kept in touch with both Louise and Sally. Louise and Paul remained close, although with Pearl gone, they obviously saw less of each other.

Paul and Sally returned to their daily routines. Sally finished her book of poetry, titled *My Father, Imagined,* and found a small press happy to publish it. She also established a residency fellowship in Neurology in Noah's name at Physicians and Surgeons.

One thing that did change were their living arrangements. Sally gave up her Manhattan apartment and bought a two-bedroom co-op in a building on Lincoln Place in Park Slope, no more than a fifteen-minute walk to Paul's apartment. Although they remained single, they spent most nights together. And on Sundays, at her pace, they jogged together around Prospect Park.

On one of those runs, Sally suggested to Paul that they work on a project together – her words and his images to honor and venerate his mother's life and those of other women like her. "You know *Maus*, don't you, by Art Speigelman?" she asked.

"The Holy Grail of the graphic novel."

"Forget the mice, cats and pigs. But what if we used it as a model to tell your mother's story?"

And so they did. The next day, the two set out to create *By The Sea*. It took them two years to complete it. It's enough to note here how it begins: A panel of cartoons depicts a young woman watching a young man swimming in the ocean off of a jetty in Coney Island. She watches for a while and then follows him, as he walks out of the water, towards the boardwalk. The caption reads:

She didn't mean to stalk him. It wasn't in her nature. That's not how she had been brought up. Not this Brooklyn girl...

Acknowledgements

I want to thank my grandchildren for allowing me to "borrow" their poems. Ben Stroud wrote *The Arglefarg* when he was in elementary school. He is now a freshman at The University of Pittsburgh. Lily Stroud wrote *So This is Freedom* when she was in middle school. She is now a junior at Smith College.

I have known Tom Sobel since our freshman year at Columbia College. We have been roommates and close friends for more than a half-century. He is not responsible for any errors in punctuation, spelling or syntax that may appear in *By The Sea*. But it has only been improved by his many diligent readings and suggestions.

I also want to thank my daughter, Ruth Levine, and two old friends, Richard White and Robert Lipsyte, for their thoughtful comments. My wife, Gale, has not read a word of what I have written. But she has always been there for me in ways far more important. So, too, Ruth, my son-in-law Matt, and of course, Lily and Ben. Nor should we forget Ed, my "grand-dog," who loves me unconditionally!

About the Author

Born and raised in Brooklyn, I returned home in 2002, after a thirty-year career teaching and writing American history and directing the American Studies Program at Michigan State University. At that point in my life, I had written a number of books, including *Ellis Island to Ebbets Field: Sport and the American Jewish Experience, A.G. Spalding and the Rise of Baseball: The Promise of American Sport, Idols of the Game: A Sporting History of the American Century*(with Robert Lipsyte), and a novel, *The Rabbi of Swat*. I also had the opportunity to be a "talking head" and contributor to a host of television documentaries, including Ken Burn's *Baseball, The First Shot, American Baseball: A Love Story, and Idols of the Game* for TBS.

Since returning home, I've enjoyed a second life as a professional actor and playwright. I've appeared in over sixty plays – both in New York and in regional theatres - in both leading and supporting roles. I've also written a number of plays, two of which, *The Kitchen Table* and *Apple, Table Penny*, had successful New York runs.

www.ingramcontent.com/pod-product-compliance
Lightning Source LLC
Chambersburg PA
CBHW070553180626
46817CB00005B/1817